LOVE IN BLOOM

Karen Rose Smith

A KISMET® Romance

METEOR PUBLISHING CORPORATION
Bensalem, Pennsylvania

For my Mom and Dad.
Daddy, I hope you know.

For all those who have experienced the
emotional and physical pain of injury,
I wish you the courage to fight and
triumph one day at a time.

KAREN ROSE SMITH

Karen Rose Smith's cat, Kasie, often sits on her lap
in their sun-filled family room as Karen writes. A
former English teacher, Ms. Smith gets her inspira-
tion from Shakespeare and Byron, but also new age
music, the farm in her backyard, and the frilly irises
in her newly landscaped garden. Residing in Pennsylvania with her husband Steve and son Ken, she uses
local settings for many of her books. Readers can
write to Ms. Smith at P. O. Box 1545, Hanover, PA
17331.

Other books by Karen Rose Smith:

No. 74   *A MAN WORTH LOVING*
No. 100   *GARDEN OF FANTASY*

ONE

The breeze blew Paige Conrad's chin-length brown hair across her cheek as she stood in the gravel lane beside her car. She couldn't take her eyes off the superbly built man cutting diagonal swipes across the wide lawn behind his home. He certainly didn't *look* as if he'd been in an accident.

Perspiration molded his shirt to his body as he drove the riding mower. He wore the plaid cotton open down the front, and the material flew out behind him on the turns, teasing her with glimpses of a strong bronzed chest—

Suddenly, out of nowhere, a furry, smelly, black-and-tan animal leaped up and pushed Paige against the car. She didn't have time to scream as her hands came up to protect her face. Pictures flashed through her mind. Pictures of lions roaming the veld. Searching for their next meal. Her hands shook. Her whole body trembled. Her legs didn't feel as if they'd hold her up. . . .

A wet, sloppy tongue licked her chin. She took a breath. A lion would *not* be licking her face.

"Shep! Down!"

Paige peeped through her fingers.

The dog's ears pricked up. With his paws still on her shoulders, he stopped licking and cocked his head toward the strong baritone.

Afraid to move in case sudden motion would change the dog's friendliness to a nip or bite, Paige stood still and concentrated on her breathing as the buzz of the mower ceased and the voice came closer.

"*Now*, Shep. Off of her."

The dog moved aside and sat at Paige's feet. She closed her eyes again and took a final, deep, tremulous breath of relief.

"Are you all right?"

Paige thought she'd steadied her racing pulse. But at the sight before her, it galloped again. The flaps of Clayton Reynolds's shirt gaped open and a hard, muscular, hair-covered chest blocked her field of view. This was not the way she'd envisioned the two of them meeting.

He backed up to offer her his hands, and she realized she was still slumped against the car. Automatically she reached for his grip. He was as strong as he was tall. She felt heat and calluses and a strange sensation as she looked at him at close range.

His black hair was shaggy and thick as if he had no interest in the latest cut. Yet it was inordinately attractive when paired with his firm jaw and high cheekbones. He looked rugged and capable of doing anything he tried, mowing down any obstacle in his way.

Few men had ever made her take a second look. In the foreign countries where she'd traveled and worked with her parents, getting involved had been a cultural taboo. When she'd attended med school in the States, she'd been too busy to look or to care. Clayton Reynolds and his piercing green eyes demanded a second look, and a third.

"Are you all right?" he repeated.

She pulled in a bolstering breath and smelled fresh-mown lawn and man. "I'm fine. He just knocked the air out of me."

"I'm sorry if he scared you. He's overly friendly but harmless. By the way, I'm Clay Reynolds." He released his hold on her.

Her knees still wobbled a little from her scare. At least she assumed it was from the scare. "Paige Conrad. I'm taking over Doc Janssen's practice while he recuperates."

The German shepherd suddenly flopped at her feet and rolled over so she could rub his stomach. She stooped, brushing the soft fur gently. Shep's paws spread farther apart. Paige laughed, a sound that surprised her. In Africa, there hadn't been much to laugh about.

"He's getting what he wants already. He has a knack with women," Clay said with wry amusement.

Paige's English boarding-school upbringing left her at a disadvantage, especially on a casual basis with American men. She'd discovered that fact in med school.

Not knowing exactly how to respond to Clay's comment, she patted Shep's stomach, straightened, and pushed her hands into her jeans pockets. "Knock them over, then fall at their feet? That sounds like a tribal mating ritual."

"Doc told me about you." Clay's eyes swept over her in an appraising male way. "He said you'd been out of the States for a few years. I didn't know you were a *young* doctor. You haven't been around when I've mown Doc's lawn."

Paige felt embarrassed by Clay's perusal, though it was subtly appreciative rather than leering. She glanced toward his home, a two-story farmhouse that looked many decades old, yet sturdy and well kept. "Sometimes I get tied up in the office into the evening. Doc misses doing the yard work himself."

Clay hooked his thumb through his belt loop. "He'll be back at it soon. Doc's a tough old bird. I predict he'll be tending his irises and entering his roses in the flower show at the end of the summer."

Clay was the first person Paige had talked to who didn't think that Doc would be laid up for months. "I try to keep him from doing too much. That's important only two months after bypass surgery. But he'll be able to do more and more as weeks go by."

Clay smiled again. "C'mon inside. I have iced tea in the fridge."

"Iced tea sounds good." Paige was thankful Clay was friendly. That would make her request easier. She'd found mostly friendliness and welcome in Langley during the two months she'd been back in the States. Doc had always told her this part of Maryland was noted for it.

As she passed the flower bed along the front porch, she stopped to take in a whiff of hyacinths. Bending, she reverently touched the petal of a daffodil. "This flower bed's beautiful. Those are candytuft in the front, aren't they?" The budding green border would soon be alive with lacy snow-white blooms.

"You know your flowers."

She laughed again. "How can I know Doc and not know flowers? Actually since I've been here, I found out I really enjoy working in Doc's gardens. I planted the two gardens out front so they'll bloom summer and fall. There's something about digging in the earth and having the sun on my hair that's . . . soothing."

Clay propped one booted foot on the first porch step and rested his hand on the white banister. "How long have you known Doc?"

"Practically all my life. He and my dad were friends in med school. He's always been sort of a cross between an uncle and a grandfather." She wasn't here to discuss her background but to seek Clay's help with a patient. Taking another appreciative whiff of hyacinths, she said, "I love the beginning of May when gardens come alive."

"Spring's a rebirth."

He said it as if he'd experienced a rebirth himself. She looked into his steady green eyes and thought about her own need for renewal—her reason for coming to Langley.

They entered the old farmhouse and cooler air greeted

them from inside. The rooms looked freshly plastered and painted. Paige wondered if Clay had done the work himself.

She followed him through the living room with its stone fireplace, Navajo rugs, and tweedy blue furniture to the large country kitchen. The oak cabinets and almond counter added to the warmth of the sunshine pouring in through the double windows over the sink.

She ran her fingers over the back of one of the oak chairs sitting at a round pedestal table. "This is beautiful workmanship."

"A fellow I know in Westminster makes them. All handcrafted." Clay went to the refrigerator. He nodded to the cabinet over the counter that divided the working area of the kitchen from the dining area. "Glasses are up there."

Opening a stranger's cupboard didn't seem so strange. She was used to packing up, moving on, settling in a village for a short time, using whatever was at hand. She took two glasses and set them on the counter.

As Clay poured the iced tea, his eyes met hers. Her heart skipped a beat. She took the glass he offered and sipped at it, forcing herself to concentrate on her reason for being here.

Moving to the table, she sat down. Shep came over and lay down at her feet. "You're probably wondering why I'm here."

"It's not just a friendly visit?" Clay's green eyes twinkled, setting her insides fluttering.

Was he flirting with her? She smiled tentatively. "Not exactly. I came to ask a favor."

"Does Doc need more help around the house? I know he has problems with that one rain gutter with all those trees close by."

She loved Doc's log home in the woods. "No, it's not Doc. I'm concerned about one of his patients, Ben Hockensmith."

Clay showed no sign of recognition.

"He was in an accident about five months ago. He was riding his bike along the highway when a car hit him."

Clay's eyes lost their sparks of humor and became opaque. She couldn't tell if he'd heard about the accident or not. He folded his hands in front of him and waited for her to continue.

"Ben's had a rough time of it. He's seventeen and was headed for a football scholarship. All that's changed. He's done with specialists except for physical therapy, so he's back in our care."

"Yours and Doc's."

"Yes. And physically, Ben's doing well. Thank God he wore a helmet."

The nerve in Clay's jaw twitched and he shifted in his chair.

"But his left leg is still weak, and he has to use a cane. We're hoping he won't need that in a few months."

Shep rubbed his nose against Paige's leg. She patted his head, but that wasn't enough attention. He stood, loped over to Clay, and sat beside him. Clay scratched Shep around the neck and moved his hand down his back.

When Clay didn't ask any questions, Paige pushed on. "Ben's attitude is poor. He's in the 'why me?' stage. I've tried talking to him, encouraging him, prodding him, but it doesn't seem to help. So I talked with Doc about it and he suggested I see you."

Clay pushed back his chair, stood, and went to the counter for the pitcher of iced tea. His glass was still half full. "How does Doc expect me to help . . . Ben, is it?"

She nodded and waited, hoping Clay would sit again.

He didn't. He filled his glass, set down the pitcher, then leaned against the counter, one ankle crossed over the other. The silence in the kitchen was broken only by the ticktock of the ceramic clock on the wall.

Paige pushed her glass aside, not encouraged by the signals he was sending out. "Doc told me you were in an accident a few years back and you had to overcome some disabilities. I'd like you to talk to Ben."

Clay was quiet for a moment. "I don't see how that would do any good. I'm not a professional. There are therapists and counselors who specialize in helping with rehabilitation. Doc would have the names of good people, if not in Langley, in Baltimore."

Paige's hands fluttered as she spoke. "But you went through it yourself." She didn't know exactly what he'd gone through, but it must have been serious enough for Doc to suggest Clay talk to Ben.

Clay shook his head. "I doubt if I went through the same thing as this young man."

Her gaze took a clinical path over his body this time and saw nothing but vibrant good health. "Doc didn't tell me specifics, but apparently you've recovered from whatever happened."

Clay uncrossed his ankles and pushed away from the counter. "It looks that way, doesn't it?"

"You haven't?"

His face showed no emotion. "Not all scars are visible."

"I know that. That's why I want you to talk to Ben."

"No."

Just for a moment, she glimpsed a flash of pain in Clay's eyes. What kind of pain, she couldn't tell. "Just like that?" she asked quietly. "Without hearing any more?" She stood and stepped closer to him. She hadn't expected an out-and-out "No" any more than she'd expected her heartbeat to quicken when she stood within a foot of him. "Why can't you just talk to him?"

"I'm thirty-five years old. He's sixteen. I wouldn't know what to say."

"You were a teenager once. Surely you can remember—"

Clay turned away from her and returned the pitcher of iced tea to the refrigerator, a sign that his hospitality had come to an end. "Dr. Conrad, I'm sure you're ingenious enough to find someone who can help this teenager—really help him. I might do more harm than good."

She waited till Clay faced her. "You won't even think about it?"

He met her gaze directly. "There's nothing to think about. Now, if you'll excuse me, I have the backyard to mow. I'll walk you to your car."

Clay stood on the porch and watched Paige Conrad's blue compact car ease slowly away from the gravel onto the road. She was either a careful driver or not used to driving an automatic transmission. A pretty woman, too. Not a head-turner though, not the type of woman he would have gone for once.

At least that's what his sister Trish would tell him. But his mind wasn't on his sister; it was on Dr. Conrad.

She was at least five-feet-ten but, from the looks of it, not aware of her height. She didn't slouch or hunch her shoulders. And because she didn't, her breasts had pushed at her blue oxford shirt. He'd appreciated every curve.

Her outfit had been nondescript—blue shirt, blue jeans, sneakers that looked as if they'd been comfortable for a long time. It was the kind of outfit someone who was used to blending in wore. The idea intrigued him. He had his own reasons for camouflage and wondered about other people's.

Calling on the memory he'd honed carefully since his accident ten years ago, he pictured the exact moment he'd held out his hands to Paige. He'd been caught by the blue of her eyes. A deep, mysterious blue that seemed too dramatic for the straight brown hair that was layered to curve toward her cheeks and emphasize her oval face. Her accent added to the mystery.

He wanted to believe the tightening in the pit of his stomach had more to do with her suggestion that he talk to Ben Hockensmith rather than man-woman attraction. But he was too old to lie to himself.

Shep whined at his side. Clay crouched down and scratched the dog around his neck. "I wish I could help her, Shep."

The German shepherd rubbed against Clay's hand.

Clay had pieced his life together slowly, inch by precious inch. The three years of rehabilitation after the accident had tested every iota of endurance he'd possessed. During the past seven years in Langley, he'd learned he could have a normal life without questions, recriminations, and odd looks. The only way he could go forward was not to look back.

Ben Hockensmith might make him relive the anguish.

Paige's voice echoed in his head. "You were a teenager once. Surely you remember—"

He wished to God he could. But he never would.

"I don't understand why he won't help." Paige paced Doc's living room, unable to calm down after her encounter with Clay. She was unsettled by more than his refusal to see Ben. Something about the man himself affected her.

Doc put aside the medical journal he'd been reading. Shoving his tortoiseshell glasses on top of his head, he confessed, "I guess I should have warned you. Clay's a private person. Sociable as all get-out, but overstep the boundary and he gets as quiet as the dead of night."

"It would be so easy for him to talk to Ben. . . ."

"How do you know?"

She stopped in the center of the multicolored braided rug. "What do you mean?"

"It might not be easy for Clay."

"Exactly what happened to him?"

"I know some of his story, but it's his to tell, not mine. I wouldn't be betraying any confidence to say it was a rock-climbing accident. He's told several people that."

She paced back and forth again. "How can he *not* want

to help Ben?'' She'd had one goal in life, to learn her parents' skills so she could heal. The problem was she hadn't been able to heal well enough. She didn't want to fail with Ben, and she knew she needed help.

Doc pushed the lever on his recliner and lowered the footrest. ''Not everyone is as selfless as you and your parents. Some people don't devote their lives to looking for ways to help others.''

''Clay Reynolds is selfish?''

''I didn't say that. Sometimes our health, physical or mental, depends on thinking of ourselves first.''

''I suppose I was thinking of myself when I came here,'' she confessed.

Doc's expression was wry. ''Taking over my practice is not selfishness.''

Paige sighed and sat on the soft cushions of the sofa. She ran her fingers over one of the pheasants printed on the arm. ''I fell apart in Ethiopia. That's not easy to face. I'm a doctor. I should be able to handle—''

''Famine and poverty? Babies dying from malnutrition? Hour after hour, day after day, year after year? You were there three years, Paige, without a break. What did you expect to happen? Did you think you could neglect your own needs, your mental health, and *not* fall apart?''

''My mother hasn't.'' Paige couldn't remember when her mother had shown a weakness of any kind.

''Ah, your mother. You think she's a saint. And she might be. But we all aren't cut out for sainthood.''

Doc had never talked this way before and Paige was surprised. ''You sound like you don't approve.''

The older man's eyes were sad. ''It's not that I don't approve. But you didn't belong over there as a child, any more than you belonged stuck in a boarding school during your formative years. Your father would be alive today if he'd taken a break now and then.''

Always ready to defend the two people she idolized,

Paige responded softly, "We took furloughs to get supplies. We came back to the States once a year."

"Even when you came here with your parents, they were planning and organizing the entire time. Those weren't vacations, Paige."

"They were following their dream—to heal the world together. And now Mother's keeping that dream alive."

"But is it *your* dream?"

Paige rested her head against the back of the sofa and closed her eyes. "I thought it was. Growing up, watching them care for people, no matter what the conditions were. I thought I wanted that life, too. That's why I became a doctor."

"And now?"

"I just don't know. But I have a couple of months to figure it out."

"You know you can stay with me as long as you need to, even when I'm back on my feet. I promised your father I'd look after you."

Paige opened her eyes and sat up straight. "And you've always done a good job. I wouldn't have gotten through med school without your moral support, let alone my residency after Daddy had his stroke—" Her voice caught. Although it had been five years, Paige still missed her dad deeply. But she considered herself lucky to have Doc.

She didn't speak about her feelings easily, maybe because of her upbringing. Showing someone how she felt had always been easier than talking about it. So she changed the subject. "What would you like for supper tonight? Curried chicken or baked haddock?"

Doc's gaze was sympathetic, as if he knew talking about her father was still painful. "I think the baked haddock would be easier on my stomach." He sat forward on the recliner and put his glasses on the end table. "So what are you going to do about Ben?"

Paige hopped to her feet and started toward the kitchen.

"I'll make sure I keep an eye on him. I haven't given up on Clay Reynolds."

"Give him some time, child. Let him think about your idea. Maybe he'll come around. In fact . . . there's a square dance Saturday night at Phelps's place. I bet Clay will be there."

Paige stopped and turned around. "You think socializing with him will bring him around?"

"I think you should follow your instincts and see how set he is about keeping his life to himself. And remember that old proverb—'you catch more flies with honey than vinegar.' "

Doc couldn't mean . . . "You're not suggesting I put on makeup and bat my eyelashes, are you?"

"A little makeup wouldn't hurt." At her affronted look, he chuckled. "Not that you need it. You're as pretty as one of my white irises. But it would do you good to dress up, be with people your own age, and have some fun."

She'd spent most of her life with adults, except for the years in boarding school. Competition in med school hadn't fostered friendships or relaxation. Could Doc know exactly how inexperienced she was with men? No. She'd never talked to him about that, or to her mother, either, for that matter.

She'd come to Langley to get perspective on her life and make decisions about her future. Maybe a little fun could help her along.

Paige sat beside Doc at a picnic table in the Phelps's barn. "Are you okay sitting here? We could bring in a lawn chair from the car."

"I'm fine. We'll stay an hour or so, then head home. I still get tired so damn fast. Oh, and I want to warn you that Ron Murphy will be seeking you out tonight. He's looking for volunteers for—"

Paige didn't hear the rest of what Doc said because Clay Reynolds strode through the door. He wore a gray-and-black plaid shirt, the sleeves rolled above his forearms. His arms were as tanned as his face and spoke of many hours outdoors. He moved like an athlete, with purpose and fluidity. She remembered the sight of his solid chest, the curling black hair. . . . Her heart raced.

She watched him closely, trying to learn more about him. He seemed to know everyone. She supposed most of the people he talked to were his customers. Doc had told her Clay owned a store that sold mowers, garden equipment, and supplies.

But then again, he sure knew a lot of women. That easy grin. Even from here she could tell his green eyes sparkled with friendliness. Maybe more than friendliness, she thought, as he dropped his arm around a blonde's shoulders and gave her a quick hug. Was he involved with someone? She frowned. Why should she care if he was?

Doc leaned over. "Clay coached Little League the past couple of years. She's one of the boys' mothers."

Heat rushed to Paige's cheeks because Doc had caught her looking. "I'm just trying to find out what kind of man he is."

"You might have to strike up a conversation for that." Doc pointed to the wooden platform at the rear of the barn where musicians had gathered. "They're startin' up."

Paige couldn't see over the heads at the tables, but she heard a bow dance across a fiddle, a pick strum a guitar, and the resounding vibrations of a bass viol. Her foot tapped to the beat.

Doc nudged her arm. "Go on. Go have fun."

She hesitated. "I don't know how to square dance."

"That's something we'll have to fix," a low voice said behind her.

Recognizing the voice, she looked over her shoulder. Suddenly she was tongue-tied. She'd thought Clay would avoid her if he saw her, not seek her out. Then again, maybe he'd just come over to say hi to Doc.

Clay smiled. "Is this your first square dance?"

She flipped her leg over the bench, straddling it. "Yes. I've never even watched square dancing, let alone tried it."

"I'll partner you if you'd like to try. Joe starts out slow for the beginners," Clay encouraged. "He'll tell you what to do and how to do it. You'll catch on in no time."

"I won't make a fool of myself?"

Clay's brows lifted wickedly. "Not if *I'm* your partner."

She laughed and it felt good. She couldn't remove her gaze from Clay's, and her heart jumped.

He held out his hand, his smile giving her the confidence she needed to do something new in the midst of strangers in an unfamiliar place. Her parents and her skills had given her that confidence in the past. A man's smile never had.

She took his hand and walked beside him to the cleared floor.

Clay stood beside her as the caller requested one large circle. His elbow was at least two inches from her upper arm, but she was aware of his broad shoulders, his lean waist, his long legs encased in the black denim. The jeans were snug across his thighs and she imagined the muscles underneath were taut and powerful. How had he been injured in the accident? What had he recovered from?

The caller asked them to position themselves boy-girl, boy-girl, and described a few basic moves—do-si-do, alle-mande, bow to your partner. Then he tapped his foot and took the microphone from its holder.

The music started and Paige took a deep breath.

Clay leaned toward her, his shoulder brushing hers. "If you get lost, watch everybody else. We'll all be doing the same thing at the same time. Just relax and enjoy yourself."

To her surprise, she did. Listening to the caller, she watched Clay for signals. He *was* a good partner, grabbing her hand, nudging her shoulder to turn her in the right direction, guiding her with his eyes. She found herself smiling and finally laughing with the sheer joy of the physical activity, the appreciation of friendly neighbors having a good time together, the earthy feeling of the wooden barn with its lingering scent of hay.

Paige didn't have a problem following the caller until he sang for the women to form a circle on the inside, the men a circle on the outside.

Allemande took on new meaning. Clay skillfully clasped her arm. Her fingers met his hot skin, the wavy black hairs on his forearm. His touch on her, her touch on him seemed personal and intimate, and she felt as though she was standing still although her feet were moving.

He passed by her once, making his way around the circle. He passed by her twice. Each lap around intensified her sensitivity to him. She didn't notice any of the other men. But when she clasped Clay's arm, when he held her, she felt startled and breathless.

After the fourth lap, he pulled her to his side. His body was hot and hard.

"What are you—"

"We're supposed to promenade. Just let me lead."

She must have missed the call. Held beside Clay, with him setting the rhythm, her hands enclosed in his, she realized why her attention wasn't on the caller. There was chemistry between her and Clay, chemistry she'd always read about but had never experienced.

At the end of the song, she felt dizzy, and not from dancing in a circle. Clay guided her toward the punch bowl and filled two cups. He handed her one.

His brows arched. "Well? Did you like it?"

"The dancing?"

His lips twitched up. "Yes."

She felt her cheeks flush. "It was fun. Do they have these dances often?"

Clay took a few swallows of punch. "Not on this large

a scale. There are square-dancing clubs across the county.''

Paige brushed her bangs across her forehead and wondered if she looked as hot as she felt. Watching Clay's lips as he talked made her feel hotter. ''Do you belong to any? You seem to know what you're doing.''

''I don't have the time.''

She wondered what he did with his time, how he spent it, whom he spent it with. ''Because of the store?''

''Mostly.''

He obviously wasn't going to say more. She had a feeling getting personal information from Clay would be much more difficult than learning to square dance. But she wanted more information. For Ben's benefit, of course. Draining her punch cup, she set it down. Since Clay had approached her, maybe he'd had a change of heart about Ben. Doc had advised her to give Clay time, but . . .

''Have you given any consideration to my request?''

Clay's eyes grew darker. ''I gave you my answer when you asked.''

''You haven't thought about changing it?''

''I've thought about it.''

''And?''

Clay's voice was firm, low, and sure. ''I think someone else can do the boy more good than I can.''

''Maybe you're underestimating your ability to help.''

Clay felt a weight settle on his heart. He'd experienced the rebirth he'd mentioned to Paige; every minute of that rebirth had been painful. No one but his family knew how painful. He couldn't stir it up and escape unscathed. He'd approached Paige tonight against his better judgment. The tilt of her head and the wealth of emotions flittering across her face as she'd spoken with Doc had drawn him to her step-by-step. But that wouldn't change the way he felt about her request.

''Ben will do better with a professional who knows about—''

"Clay. Just the man I want to see." Ron Murphy clapped Clay on the shoulder. "And Dr. Conrad. I've been looking for you, too. How would you two like to work on the Fourth of July Celebration committee? We're late getting started this year and can use all the help we can get."

TWO

Clay swerved his gaze from Paige to Ron. The people of Langley had been good to him—friendly, accepting, respectful of his privacy because he kept a tight lid on what he said and whom he said it to. So he liked to give back to the community any way he could. "What does the committee do exactly?"

Ron nudged his black Stetson farther back on his head. "Runs the day. Makes sure everything's where it's supposed to be when it's supposed to be there. I need to get enough volunteers so no one person has to do too much. Everyone's busy. What do you say, Clay? Will you at least come to the meeting next week?"

Since he wasn't coaching Little League this year, he had some time. "Sure, I'll come. If there's any way I can help out, I'll be glad to. Fourth of July last year was a great success, wasn't it?"

"Darn tootin', it was. And we'll do even better this year. How about you, Dr. Conrad? Will you help out?"

Clay saw the doubts on her face and wondered where they came from and why they were there. "It'll be a great chance for you to get to know more people in Langley."

"I don't know if I have the time to spare."

24

Clay didn't believe time was the problem. He suspected she had an underlying reason for being hesitant to join in, but he wasn't willing to pry. "It's your call."

Ron Murphy was looking at her expectantly.

Reluctantly, she agreed. "All right. I'll come to the meeting and see what's involved."

Ron thanked both of them, told them he'd be in touch, and moved on to another group of neighbors. Paige picked up her cup from the table and filled it again.

"Did we back you into a corner?" Clay asked.

She smiled. "No. I would like to get more involved in the community. It's just . . ."

He arched a brow but didn't push.

"It will make it that much harder to leave if I do."

Now he understood. If she got attached, it would be more difficult to break away. "How long will you be here?"

"Two more months, maybe. Until Doc can take over again."

"And then what?"

"I'll probably go back to Africa."

The idea of her leaving caused a ripple of consternation Clay didn't understand. Just as he didn't understand why he'd encouraged her to join the committee. Why should he care? Because she obviously cared about so many things—Doc and Ben Hockensmith being at the top of her list.

There was a determination about Paige, but there was a fragility, too. Gut feeling told him it had more to do with innocence than weakness. Innocence in a woman of twenty-eight . . . thirty?

The music was going strong again, new squares were forming. "Are you going to join in?"

Paige looked toward Doc. "No. Doc's probably ready to go."

Clay nodded. It was best she wasn't staying. Their dancing had made him feel alive, filled with an energy he couldn't remember feeling as far back as he *could* remember. But he knew that feeling could cause trouble. "Tell Doc I'll be out Thursday evening to trim the hedge instead of Wednesday. My assistant manager will be gone all day and I'll be at the store late."

Paige gave him a smile that brought out the dimple in her right cheek as she lightly touched his arm. "Thanks for the dancing lessons. You *are* a good partner."

She was a woman who liked to touch. He remembered the way she'd willingly taken his hands at the car, the way she'd run her hand over his oak chair. He supposed touching was natural in a nurturing profession, but when she touched him . . . "You were an easy student to teach. I'm glad you had fun."

She removed her hand from his arm. "I might see you Thursday."

He nodded, knowing it was better if he didn't see her at all.

Paige turned away and crossed to Doc's table.

Clay mowed his fingers through his hair. She was a sweet, caring woman and he was too attracted to her. Attraction hadn't been a problem the past few years. He'd acted on it, within limits, and received satisfaction. But in this instance, attraction could only lead to complications. His aim in life now was to keep it simple. And he would.

Tuesday evening after Clay had locked his store for the day, he watched his sister sitting at the desk in his office. It was hard to believe he used to be as fascinated by numbers as she was.

Trish switched off his computer and turned the swivel chair toward him. "As usual, everything looks fine. Your business is booming. The way you've taken to management is amazing. What kind of ads are you running?"

"Eye-catching ones."

"There's more to it than that."

"Service. My customers like knowing the owner, coming to me if they have a problem. And if they know I've worked on the equipment . . . they feel like I'm one of them, not some highbrow store owner who doesn't give two hoots about service, just the products he sells."

"Sure you don't want to go into public-relations work? We could use you in the marketing department."

."Ah, Trish. What am I going to do with you? Can't you believe I'm happy here, either?"

She pushed her blond waves away from her face. "I believe it."

Trish had been Clay's ballast during his recovery. His mother had unceasingly cared for him and retaught him. But she had a tendency to overprotect. His dad had kept a cool distance. But Trish had taught him how to be a person again. He'd felt love for his sister before he'd felt it for anyone else.

He asked, "How's work?"

"You mean how's Dad, don't you?"

"Do I?"

"Gee, I've taught you how to fence well."

Clay couldn't suppress his smile. "You think you know me."

"Of course I know you. I helped develop your personality. That's why you're the fun guy you are today."

Trish teased him, but there was always an element of truth hanging in their sparring. "And Dad wishes that was different. He'll never understand I'm not the same person I was ten years ago and I never will be."

Trish frowned. "I think he still hopes you'll come back into the business."

"I can't."

"I know. I've told him over and over that your mind works differently now, that you don't enjoy designing high-tech heating systems."

"He feels he paid for me to become an electrical engineer and that's what I should be. I guess the way he sees it, his investment went down the tubes." Clay crossed to the small window in his office and looked out. "I can't explain the satisfaction that working with my hands gives me. Whether it's tearing down and rebuilding a mower or chopping wood for the fireplace. Dad sees me in work clothes and shudders. His idea of heaven is seeing everybody wearing three-piece suits."

Trish's voice was hesitant. "Does it bother you that I work with Dad and you don't?"

Clay faced his sister. He'd analyzed himself from here to next year and had faced up to the problems with his father. "You're an accountant and doing what you like, what you were trained to do. You're also doing what Dad wants, so he leaves the rest of your life alone."

"He always hated your rock climbing because of the danger involved, but he respected it because you pursued it with the same intensity you pursued anything. But when you told him you were moving to Langley and setting up your own business, it shot his plans to smithereens."

Clay's father had a problem with not being in control of his son's life. "You're the only one who understands why I had to get away from Reisterstown."

"Yes, I do. But you didn't answer my question. Does seeing me work for Dad bother you?"

He'd been honest with Trish in everything up to this point. "No, his lack of understanding bothers me. If you decided to put your accounting degree aside to become a chef, you'd have the same problems with him that I have."

"Maybe. But it's worse for you because you're his son, the male he presumed would carry on his business and his name."

Clay grinned. "Forget the business . . . now the name could be easier—"

Trish laughed. "Your sense of humor is much more developed this time around."

"Without it, I couldn't have survived." Clay swung

Trish's swivel chair in a circle until she giggled and put her hand on his arm to stop him. He held the arm of the chair. "Enough of this serious stuff. I'm going horseback riding this weekend. Want to come along?"

Her brown eyes gleamed with mischief. "What if I make you a deal?"

Clay let go of the chair and stood up straight. "Uh-oh. I usually get the short end of your deals."

She made a face at him. "I'll go horseback riding with you Saturday if you come to Mom and Dad's for a barbecue on Sunday."

"That's a steep trade-off."

"Mom misses you."

"I know. I talked to her last week."

"And you can put up with Dad for a couple of hours."

"That's your opinion."

"I'd really like you to be there, Clay."

He stopped treating her request lightly. "What's happening?"

Her expression became coy. "If I tell you that, it won't be a surprise."

"Trish . . ."

"Just say you'll come. It's important to me."

After all she'd done for him, he couldn't say no.

Paige pulled her black bag from her car Thursday evening after paying a visit to one of Doc's elderly patients who couldn't drive. She was supposed to take off Thursdays, but she used them to catch up. Glancing at the red-and-white Blazer sitting in Doc's drive, she realized she'd seen it before, parked in Clay's gravel lane. She listened but didn't hear the sound of the mower or hedge trimmer.

She let herself in the front door. The wooden screen door slapped behind her. "Doc?"

No answer.

Going into the kitchen, she peered out the side window and saw the door to the storage shed was open. Investigating, she found Clay on the floor, sitting to the side of the mower.

Doc handed him a wrench. Seeing Paige in the doorway, he smiled. "Hi, there. The mower's been stalling, so Clay wanted to check it out."

Clay shifted his body toward her. His perusal made her feel . . . naked. Why? Men had looked at her before. But Clay was different; her reactions to him confused her. She certainly wasn't wearing anything provocative. Her forest-green slacks and beige blouse were not fashion's finest. She wore a lab coat over her clothes most of the day, so what was underneath didn't much matter—as long as it was clean, pressed, and conservative. Yet Clay seemed to see deeper than clothes, maybe even deeper than skin.

"Busy day?" he asked easily, his deep husky voice vibrating through her, as he turned back to the mower and tightened a bolt.

"Aren't they all?" Clay's presence in the shed was disconcerting. To feel as if she were on solid ground, she said to Doc, "I had three cases of poison ivy. Kids can't wait to put on shorts and go exploring."

"The lake was crowded last Sunday with boaters and fishermen. Adults are just as eager to get outdoors," Clay commented, his attention on the machine before him.

"Clay canoes on the lake," Doc explained.

"Early evening's best. When all the activity's calmed down."

He canoed, danced, did physical labor. Whatever had happened in the accident, he seemed to be completely recovered now. But then he'd mentioned scars that weren't visible. How deep did they run? "Canoeing on the lake sounds nice."

Clay glanced at her. "You can come out with me some evening if you'd like."

Alone. With Clay Reynolds. On a lake at dusk. A shiver ran up Paige's back. Before she thought better of it, she responded, "I'd like that." She studied Clay's hands. They were large. She could still remember their warm grip when he'd helped her away from her car, as he held her when they danced. She could imagine him in a canoe, his strong arms paddling.

Clay asked, "When's your day off?"

"I don't have office hours Thursdays or Sundays, but I usually go to the hospital and see my patients in the morning. Then I'm free."

Doc shut the toolbox. "I thawed out those chicken breasts like you said. Want me to start the grill?"

"Sure. Clay, have you had supper yet?"

He slid back a foot from the mower. "No. I'm going to grab something on the way home."

"You're welcome to stay."

"Believe me, son, it'll be *good* for you. Paige keeps me on a strict diet."

Clay climbed to his feet and wiped his hands on the towel on the mower's seat. "I don't want to impose."

"It's no imposition." As she crossed to the door, her heart sped up at the idea of spending more time with Clay. "You'll keep Doc and me from talking shop."

Clay watched through the doorway as Paige's slim legs took her to the house. "Does she ever slow down?"

"Afraid to is my guess."

That gave Clay pause. "Afraid of what?"

"Afraid of what she might find out about herself if she does."

Clay stood inside the sliding glass doors in the dining room. The cedar deck extended from the dining room on stilts. The ground underneath was rocky and uneven. Doc had decided not to landscape it, to keep it natural. The steps descended to an uneven packed-earth walk that led into the woods.

Paige stood at the grill against the back of the house and basted the chicken. Clay knew he shouldn't have invited her to go for a canoe ride on the lake, but it would have been rude not to. He could picture too easily how she'd look with the moon on her hair and the intimacy of darkness settling around them, an intimacy that opened the door to exchanging confidences. She'd tell him why she'd come to Langley; he'd explain . . .

No. If he took her for a canoe ride, it would be in broad daylight with other boaters around. He wasn't trading secrets with Paige Conrad.

He opened the sliding door and stepped outside. "Ron Murphy called and said the committee meeting is eight o'clock next Tuesday. You going?" Clay asked.

Paige glanced at him, then back down at the grill. "I said I would."

He bet she was the type of person who always followed through on her promises. "Where did you grow up? You have a unique accent."

She smiled. "I never noticed."

He smiled back. Some of her words were enunciated too precisely, sometimes the rhythm seemed unusual. "How long have you been away from the States?"

"Most of my life. Half anyway."

"Where have you lived?"

"We lived in western Pennsylvania till I was three. Then we went to Central America. When I was ten, my parents sent me to a boarding school in England. At sixteen, I went to be with them in Zambia. I came back here for college and med school in Ohio. When I finished my residency, I joined my mother in Ethiopia."

She'd given him her rundown dispassionately, as if she'd had to do it often. "Just your mother?"

She hesitated, and her eyes clouded. "My father died when I was doing my residency."

Now that was a subject she wasn't dispassionate about. Her sadness touched him. "I'm sorry."

Paige turned away. After a moment, she asked, "What about you? Is your family here?"

"In Reisterstown. I moved here seven years ago when I heard the store I now own was up for sale."

"Do you see them often?"

"My sister, I do."

"I always wondered what a normal family would be like."

The wistfulness in her voice intrigued him. "What do you call normal?"

She stared into the treetops as if she could envision it exactly. "Living in one place for years, building friendships, going to a regular school."

He wished he could remember if his childhood had been "normal." His family said it had. "You were lonely?" He was no stranger to loneliness and recognized it when he heard it.

"Holidays were the hardest," she confessed. "Especially in boarding school. The other girls went home. I couldn't contact Mom and Dad because they moved from village to village."

Clay could see the lonely little girl who had no place to go and wondered why the hell she didn't resent her parents. He didn't hear resentment. "Didn't your parents worry about you, try to contact you?"

"Oh, they sent boxes of presents they ordered. And wrote constantly. It wasn't so bad." She flipped the chicken to the platter.

When Clay reached for it to put it on the table, so did she. Their fingers touched. Their eyes met.

After a moment, she pulled back. He watched as her face pinkened, knowing he'd like to stroke her cheek and hold her in his arms. She had a freshness, a naturalness that connected with basic needs inside him. But he knew better than to act on them with this woman.

Paige set the dish on the table. Her voice was low and reminded him of long nights, a starry sky, his king-size bed. "If you'll set the table, I'll get the rice and the salad."

He dispelled the image of touching her skin, kissing her. "Will do."

Paige went inside. Clay took a deep breath.

When she returned, Doc accompanied her. She put the food on the table and as they ate, Doc guided the conversation. Clay observed Paige and wondered again about her reason for coming to Langley. Any number of doctors could have covered for Doc.

Doc winked as he popped a strawberry into his mouth. "Beats lemon meringue pie, doesn't it?"

Clay laughed. Paige smiled and her gaze met his. They shared a look that said they both cared enough about Doc to make him toe the line.

Paige gathered the plates and silverware. Clay helped and stowed the leftovers in the refrigerator. "You're spoiling Doc, you know."

"He deserves to be spoiled. He's a wonderful man."

"I remember what he *used* to eat. Hot dogs, steak, potatoes and gravy."

She chuckled. "He turned up his nose at the first few suppers I put on the table, but he's getting used to low-fat meals."

"Supper was very good."

"Thanks." She added soap to the dishwasher and closed the door. "I like to cook. I'm getting used to the microwave again and all the conveniences I haven't had for a while." She pushed the start cycle. "I usually go for a walk after supper. Would you like to join me?"

He knew every moment he spent with Paige he was getting in deeper. But being with her seemed preferable to not being with her. "Sure."

When they went back outside, Doc was settled in an old wooden rocking chair. "Can't beat May evenings."

"Did you walk today?" Paige asked.

"Twice. Almost a mile at a time, now. It felt good."

"Then you don't want to come with us for another one?"

"No. I'll wait for the moon to come up."

Paige and Clay descended the wooden steps and walked along the path until they entered a grove of tall maples, poplars, and evergreens. The packed earth muffled their footsteps. They hadn't gone far when sunlight showered them again.

Clay pointed across the clearing. "Look at that."

The sunshine played over a colorful display of violets, buttercups, and columbines. Paige stepped closer to Clay to peer around the tree trunks. "I've never seen a planned garden look more beautiful. I wish the one I planted out front could capture that free feeling."

Clay leaned against a tree trunk. "That's what I like about wild flowers. They're free, unique, and grow wherever they fall. They survive with their surroundings."

She studied him. "Are you like that?"

"I try to be." They were standing close. Too close. He could see a faint spray of freckles across the bridge of her nose.

She asked softly, "Clay, what happened to you in the rock-climbing accident?"

It was strange. He almost felt that if he could tell anyone, he could tell her. "I talk about it as little as possible, Paige."

"Why?"

He decided to be honest with her. "It's safer that way. The less people know about you, the less they can hurt you."

"I've found people usually want to help, not hurt."

Paige saw the world through her own eyes—nurturing, caring eyes—and she thought everybody else had the same vision. "In a town the size of Langley, everyone knows everyone else's business. It's not unusual. That's just the way it works. People talk. Stories stretch. Rumors fly. Tell one person, you tell the town."

She took a step back. "And you think I'd . . . gossip about you?"

She looked shocked he'd even think such a thing. He gently clasped her shoulder. "No. Not intentionally."

The ends of her hair teased his hand as she tipped up her chin. "I know what confidentiality is all about, Clay."

"I know you do." He removed his hand because he was tempted to do more than hold her shoulder. Her lips were so perfect. . . .

He looked over at the clearing of wild flowers and the sun's rays fading behind the trees. "It'll be getting dark soon."

She accepted his change of subject and gave him a sweet, soul-healing smile. "We wouldn't want to get caught in the woods after dark."

He thought of holding her close through a long dark night, woods or no woods. The wall he'd carefully constructed to keep his heart safe was starting to crack. It was an unsettling feeling. "No, we wouldn't. We might get lost."

He moved away from the tree and waited for her to join him on the path. They'd finish their walk and he'd go home, his comfortable life still intact.

_____ THREE _____

Ron Murphy held the meeting for the Fourth of July Celebration at his house in downtown Langley. Clay surveyed the group in the living room and realized he was a nodding acquaintance of most of the people there.

Then there was Paige. Standing in the woods, he'd wanted to take her in his arms, lay her down on the bed of wild flowers and . . . and nothing. Paige Conrad pounded on his defenses with both fists. She didn't even know it. That's how he knew she was vulnerable. That's why he knew he had to be careful.

Paige sat with a notebook and pen in hand. She wore no makeup and he liked the natural look. Her jeans told him she'd stopped at Doc's to change before the meeting. Her pink sweater showed her graceful neck to advantage. He'd never seen skin so perfect—like one of Doc's roses.

With determined purpose, Clay focused on what Ron was saying.

"So Martha and Rita are taking care of getting food vendors. John and Tom will make arrangements for the kiddie rides. Lou and Betsy will find flags and memorabilia and work on the decorations. Now, we need something . . . spectacular to get everyone's attention and make some money at the same time.

Middle-aged and plump Martha suggested, "We could get an adult Ferris wheel to go along with the children's rides."

Her husband, Tom, disagreed. "That will only bring in peanuts. We need a show. What about flame throwers? Or a rodeo rider doing stunts on a horse?"

Clay leaned forward. "A hot-air balloon would work. It would be unusual and still make money."

"I'll say!"

"Great idea."

"Way to go, Clay."

"If it's not too expensive," a dissenting voice added.

Ron stretched his legs out in front of him. "People will pay for something different. I heard of a guy in Lineboro who pilots one. A new resort south of here used him when they had their grand opening. I'll get his name." He turned to Clay. "You might have to drive over, see what he's got, and make arrangements."

"That's no problem."

Ron turned his attention to Paige. "Well, Dr. Conrad, that leaves one area open for you. How are you at planning games?"

"Games?"

"Yeah, you know—egg toss, relay races, that sort of thing. Think you could plan the afternoon for us?"

Paige seemed out of her depth. Clay wondered if games hadn't been a part of her life. He supposed that was possible.

She asked, "Do you have examples of what you've done in the past?"

"Naw. No one keeps notes on this stuff. But if you talk to people, they'll tell you."

"I can help her out with that," Clay offered.

"Great! So I'll put you two on the games committee."

"I didn't mean—"

Ron cut Clay off. "And I'll take care of the fireworks. Sounds like a whopper of a day to me. Okay, everybody, that's it. There's drinks and chips on the back porch."

Paige looked at Clay; Clay looked at Paige. They both laughed. Clay said, "It looks like we have a job to do. I'm tied up Thursday. Will you be free Sunday afternoon?"

"Around one."

"Do you want to ride with me to Lineboro? We can discuss games. Maybe when we get back we can take that canoe ride."

"If it's not too late."

"If it's not too late. I know you doctors need your beauty sleep."

She blushed and pushed her hair behind her ear.

He frowned. She acted as if she wasn't used to receiving compliments. "How old are you, Paige?"

Her blue eyes widened. "Twenty-nine. Why?"

"Just curious."

He stood. She rose, too, and as she came around the coffee table he could smell perfume and delicate woman.

"Before we go out with the others," she said, "I wanted to tell you I found a counselor for Ben."

Clay breathed an inaudible sigh of relief. "That's great. I know that's the right way to go."

"I hope so."

She seemed unsure, as if he would still be better suited to talking to the teenager than a professional. Clay couldn't understand why. He was relieved she'd found help for the boy. He was also relieved there was a group of people socializing on the back porch. As much as he'd like to be alone with Paige, he knew a group atmosphere would be safer.

Now, Sunday . . .

Friday afternoon, Paige settled in the chair behind her desk and read Ben Hockensmith's chart, though she didn't need to. She had it memorized. He'd seen his counselor yesterday. Paige had talked to her this morning and wasn't encouraged by what she'd heard. "Physically, you're doing superbly, Ben. Your grip strength in your left hand is normal."

Ben's brown eyes were defiant. "But my leg isn't. And it's never going to be, is it, Dr. Conrad?"

The car had hit Ben on the left, broken his left arm, but had done much more damage to the left leg. The surgeon had inserted a pin. "I can't tell you what will happen. A large part depends on you. Look how far you've come. By the end of the summer you probably won't need the cane."

"But I'll never play pro football now. I'll never get that athletic scholarship."

"There are loans, grants—"

Ben's chin jutted out as he banged his fist on the chair arm while his other tightened on his cane. "Don't you get it, Dr. Conrad? I don't *want* to do anything but play football."

"Ben . . ."

He threw his cane on the floor in disgust. "And I don't want to use a damn cane one more day. Everyone stares at me!"

"Everyone?"

With a sullen glance, he muttered, "You know what I mean. They look at me like I'm a . . . cripple." He lowered his head, his chin practically touching his chest. "Maybe I am."

Paige hated the hopelessness in the teenager's tone. She grasped at anything to say to make him feel better. "Franklin Delano Roosevelt was President of the United States and he was in a wheelchair."

Ben looked at her as if she'd suddenly grown three noses. "I don't *want* to be President of the United States. I want to play football."

Ben's major problem was he didn't want to change his view of his future, let alone his life. "Your parents tell me you get good grades. Doesn't anything else interest you?"

Ben's eyes were no longer defiant but dull and lifeless. "I started playing football with friends when I was eight years old. In junior high, I could run faster than anybody else on the team. I've practiced and played in heat and rain and mud, and I love it. Nothing . . . absolutely nothing can replace football."

She said softly, "It's not only the game, is it? As star quarterback, you received an awful lot of attention."

His smile was smug. "Girls couldn't wait to go out with me."

"But were they going out with you because you were the star quarterback or because you were Ben Hockensmith?"

The smugness faded along with the smile. "What difference does it make?"

"You tell me."

He was quiet. Finally he admitted, "I guess I was more important when I was quarterback."

"Do you want people to like you for that reason?"

Ben shifted restlessly in his chair. "I don't know. I just . . ."

"Just what?"

He stared pensively at the leg that wouldn't work as well as he wanted it to. "When I first had the accident, everybody was there. With flowers and cards and . . . just there. Then I went into rehab for a month and it was like everybody forgot I existed. And when I came home, I was a semester behind and everybody acted like the accident never happened. Like they didn't care anymore. My old friends . . . they're just not around now."

Her heart went out to him and she wanted to ease the loneliness and abandonment he felt, yet she didn't know how. "Ben, I don't know what to tell you. Change is hard for everyone. And people do get sidetracked."

"I have one friend, *one*, who still calls and comes around."

"Then he's a real friend."

"But I want to play football with the guys, hang around the sports store."

She heard the catch in his voice. "I understand how you must feel. But, Ben, you have to start over."

He raised his head and his eyes were shiny. "I don't want to start over. I want it all back."

She leaned forward. "You have to look ahead, not back."

"Now you sound like that counselor you sent me to. She doesn't understand squat."

Paige held his gaze. "Have you given her a fair chance?"

"Talking about it isn't going to change it. She wants me to take these tests."

"What kind of tests?"

He lifted one shoulder halfheartedly. "I don't know. Bunches of questions that are supposed to show what I like and what I don't."

She nodded. "Interest surveys. They're not exactly tests. They'll show where your strengths and weaknesses are, what you might be good at. If you take them, it might give you direction."

Ben pushed at his cane with his right foot and shoved it closer to his chair. "I know what I'm good at. Football."

Paige stood and went around her desk. She leaned against the front. "Will you do me a favor?"

His expression was wary. "What?"

"Do the interest surveys."

"It's not gonna do any good," he mumbled.

"Just take them and see what they say."

He surveyed Paige speculatively. "Okay. As a favor to you. You've been okay with me, Dr. Conrad. You're straight and don't feed me a line of gop that everything's going to be fine."

She had to be honest with herself and her patients to treat them effectively. That had been her big problem in Africa. She hadn't been honest with herself. Compassion and honesty had gotten rolled into one until neither was clear.

But she had to forget th?* for now. "I want everything to be fine for you, Ben. But you've got to look ahead, not back."

He shook his head dejectedly. "I don't see how."

She had to make Ben open his eyes to new possibilities, but she didn't know how. She'd bet her stethoscope Clay Reynolds did.

Paige glanced at Clay as he drove Sunday afternoon, admiring his profile. His bone structure created strong, defined lines. His jaw especially was insistently masculine. He had a way of setting it when she asked him questions he didn't want to answer.

He was relaxed today. She knew why. He didn't think she'd mention Ben again. He was wrong, but the early afternoon had been enjoyable and she didn't want to break the mood just yet. She liked being with Clay, though her reactions to him confused her. Why did she respond so strongly to him? Because she was at a crossroads in her life?

Or was it Clay himself? His strength, his gentle support, his appreciation of life. He'd been enthusiastic as he showed her the hot-air balloon. She'd seen it lying in a barn, all spread out.

As they drove back to Clay's house, she asked, "Is that wicker basket the passengers stand in really safe?"

"Randy said he's been piloting about ten years. He's never had an accident. So I wouldn't worry."

"I just thought when it comes back down to the ground, it would land hard."

"Not if it's done right. Do you think you'll try it?"

"I'm not sure."

His quick glance was puzzled. "You fly in planes, don't you?"

"Yes. But they're closed in. This is open, suspended in midair."

Clay flicked on his turn signal and passed a tractor rumbling in front of them. "Did you ever want to be a bird?"

"Not particularly."

He chuckled. "You've never sat on a hill and looked up and wondered what it would be like to soar above everything, to be free to go high and low and see the world from an entirely different perspective?"

"No. I've sat on a hill, stared out at miles of sand and dry earth and wondered what in the world I could do for these people to make their lives easier."

"You're a crusader."

"No! No, I'm not." She hated when anyone called her that. It was not meant as a compliment but more as a click of the tongue, as if she and her parents were all Don Quixotes charging at windmills.

Clay's voice was gentle. "There's nothing wrong with crusading if that's what you want to do."

He seemed sincere—sincere enough for her to want to confide her confusion about the direction of her life. But she couldn't do that. She had to solve this one herself.

Shep greeted Paige and Clay at the door when they returned to Clay's house. He stood on his hind legs, his paws on Paige's thighs.

"Shep, down," Clay commanded.

He got a tilt of the head from the dog as if he was asking, "Do you really mean it?"

Paige laughed. "It's okay." She patted Shep's side and scratched around his ears.

Clay shook his head. "I don't know what it is with him when he's around you. He usually follows commands. I take him to the store and he doesn't bother the customers."

Paige gave the animal a final pat, and the dog pushed

away. He trotted into the kitchen, heading toward the back door.

Clay went after him. "He wants to go out. We can sit at the table to talk about the games."

In the car they'd talked about the countryside, music, Doc. They hadn't gotten around to the Fourth of July. Paige followed Clay. "How long have you had Shep?"

"Since I moved here."

"I've often wanted to have a dog."

Clay opened the back door and Shep ran outside. "Another part of a normal life?"

"I guess." Someone to love that would be strictly hers. She'd always felt her parents belonged to the world, not to her in particular.

"There are lots of them that need homes. I got Shep from the SPCA."

"Did you have a dog as a boy?"

Clay paused and came over to the table. "No." He pulled a chair out and motioned for her to sit. "As soon as we plan the agenda, we can go for that canoe ride. Days like this are made for floating in the middle of the lake."

So many puzzle pieces missing where Clay was concerned. He was close-mouthed about his background, yet his friendliness was genuine. "I really know nothing about planning these games. I mean, I know what a relay race is because we did that in physical education. But that's about all I know."

"Think fun, laughter, exertion. We need something for everyone. How about a balloon toss?"

"You bat a balloon back and forth?"

He laughed and sat down across from her. "No. You fill the balloons with water and toss them back and forth to a partner. The team farthest apart wins. We could do several rounds of it, winners play winners."

"I suppose these balloons break?"

He wiggled his brows. "You bet. That's the fun part. Wet hair, wet faces, wet T-shirts—"

She imagined her shirt molded to her chest and Clay seeing it. Feeling heat rise to her cheeks, she cleared her throat. "And what do the winners get?"

He studied her face thoughtfully. "We'll decide that later. Ribbons or buttons."

"What about baked goods? You said we need something for everyone. We could have a baked-goods contest. The prize-winning entries can go to the winners of the games."

"That's an excellent idea. And maybe we could have a pie-eating contest."

"I can treat everyone with antacids after it's over."

"What else are doctors for?"

She thought about that a lot lately.

Clay reached behind the table and pulled open a drawer. Taking out paper and pen, he pushed it toward her. "You want to take notes, or should I?"

"I can." It would give her something to do so she didn't have to look into Clay's green eyes so often. They had a most disturbing effect on her.

"Three-legged races are always good," he suggested.

She wrote down their ideas.

Clay leaned back in his chair, rocking it on its two back legs. "What about a softball game? One for the kids and one for adults. Maybe we could sell T-shirts—"

Barking from out back had Clay's head swinging toward the window. Spotting Shep running across the yard after a rabbit, Clay swore, jumped up, and ran out the back door, letting the screen door slam.

Paige took off after him. The expression on his face had been grim. But she couldn't begin to keep up with Clay's long-legged stride.

Shep streaked across the yard, headed for the split-rail fence at the back boundary. Clay slowed, but when Shep curved to the right, he picked up the pace again.

Paige suddenly saw why. The stretch of fence for which Shep was headed wasn't split rail, but barbed wire. She tried to run faster to help Clay head off the German shepherd.

Clay yelled over and over, "Shep, heel. Shep, heel." But the dog paid no mind. The furry little creature scurrying in front of him held all his interest.

When the hare made a circle, trying to figure out which way was safe, Clay reached the fence before the dog. Paige thought they'd averted trouble, but the rabbit suddenly veered toward the barbed wire and so did Shep.

The rabbit dashed under the fence. Before Shep could follow, Clay tackled him.

By the time Paige arrived, Clay was playfully wrestling with the dog and scolding him at the same time. "You've got to leave the rabbits alone. They don't appreciate being scared to death by a big son-of-a-gun like you. That was probably a mama hurrying home to her babies."

Paige couldn't believe Clay wasn't yelling and swearing at the dog for the bother and fuss. There was a strong connection between him and Shep, and a caring attitude on Clay's part. In the countries where she'd lived, dogs were little more than wild animals. The villagers hadn't had enough food to feed themselves, let alone their pets.

Paige wiped her hair away from her forehead while her breathing returned to normal. Clay didn't even appear winded. Since she'd met him, she'd seen nothing to suggest he'd been injured in any way.

Shep looked beyond the fence toward the brush where the rabbit had disappeared.

Clay said firmly and loudly, "No, Shep. No."

The dog whined and gave his master a pleading look.

Clay repeated, "No."

Shep sat and cocked his head as if inquiring, "Why not?"

Clay pushed himself to a sitting position and pointed to the house. "Back home, Shep. Go home."

The dog glanced at Clay, the area beyond the fence, then back at the house. He took off in the direction of the house.

Clay moved his arm and Paige thought she saw him wince as he stood and dusted off his jeans. "I told old man Holtz this would never work. That section of fence rotted and his cows were getting out. So he rigged up the barbed wire temporarily. But there must be a nest of rabbits back there."

"Shep likes rabbits?"

"He likes the fast movement and thinks it's a game. I'm going to have to put up that length of fence myself so he doesn't get hurt. He thinks he can run under it like the rabbits do."

When Clay lifted his arm to brush loose grass from his knee, Paige saw his cut hand. "Clay, you're hurt. Let me see."

He glanced at the tricklings of blood. "It's nothing. I must have scraped it when I took Shep down."

She held his hand in hers and examined the top. "You didn't scrape it, you cut it on the barbed wire. It looks nasty. Have you had a tetanus shot recently?"

"Two years ago."

She ran her thumb over his, over the bend between it and his index finger. There were four cuts and a few scratches below his knuckles. "Do you have a first-aid kit?"

When her eyes found his, the awareness there shook her. She could feel the heat between their hands. Clay stood immobile, a deep fire glowing in his green eyes that made her excited and afraid at the same time.

He stared at their clasped hands then at her lips. He drew in a breath. "No, I don't have a first-aid kit here."

His response took a moment to register; her body felt as if it were melting under his gaze. She knew she'd better release his hand before she stepped even closer and wanted more than a simple touch.

"I have my bag in my car." She started across the yard.

While Paige fetched her bag, Clay washed his hand at the kitchen sink, amazed that he could still feel her touch under the cool water. He could tell she didn't know her comforting little touches drove him crazy. He'd almost kissed her. He'd almost wrapped his arms around her. . . .

Dear Lord, this woman got to him in more than physical ways. Once in a while, she used an unusual turn of phrase that showed she'd been out of the States. And it added to her—there was that damn word again—innocence. She even blushed!

Her exploration of his hand had been almost curious. Well, the curiosity would have to stop. So would the hot, tight ache that plagued him whenever he got too close to her. They'd finish planning games for the Fourth of July, take a quick canoe ride, and go back to being . . . neighborly.

When Paige entered the kitchen, Clay was prepared. Her soft scent wouldn't snare him, the vulnerability in her blue eyes wouldn't touch him. He'd set his mind to feats he'd thought were impossible. Defying attraction he felt for one woman should be easy.

Paige joined him at the sink, washed her hands, then opened her bag on the table. She took a gauze pad and a bottle of peroxide from inside. "Sit down over here. The light's better."

"There's really no reason why—" The determination on her face stopped him. He might as well get this over with, and quickly. He parked on the chair next to hers and laid his hand on the table.

She smiled. "You don't have to look as if I'm going to chop it off. I'll be as gentle as I can."

He knew she would. That was the problem. He steeled himself for her touch, though her smile had almost the same effect on his nervous system.

Paige talked as she prepared the wounds. "I've noticed.

Shep listens most of the time. Did you train him yourself?''

The wet gauze was cold, the light caress of her fingers warm. ''Yes. I got one of those videos. It worked well.'' He tried to ignore her thumb under his palm, holding his hand in the right position.

''You have patience.''

He had more patience with others than himself. ''Shep wants to please. It's just when a distraction or innate instincts take over that we have a problem.'' In some ways, men and dogs weren't so different.

Paige's sleek hair swung across her cheek as she leaned forward to dab at his hand with another sterile patch. The whiff of her perfume made him lean back.

He looked over her shoulder and stared at the pattern of the wallpaper on the wall behind her. ''I took him along to Reisterstown last weekend and he behaved like a gentleman. Of course, he got plenty of attention from my mother and Trish.''

''Trish is your sister?''

Clay nodded. The soreness of the cuts was nothing compared to the pain of another kind of need Paige stirred up by touching him.

''Don't you usually take him along?''

''No. I only go for short visits.''

Paige unclasped his hand and rummaged in her bag. ''You stayed all weekend?''

Clay grunted. ''No. An afternoon and evening. Trish announced her engagement, so we discussed wedding plans.''

''How nice!''

''She thinks so. I do too. Michael's a nice guy. But they've been living together for two years. I didn't know if they'd want to make it permanent.''

''Have you ever been married?''

The tension in his body made Clay say more sharply

than he intended, "No." He shifted his feet under the table. "Have you?"

Paige sat against the carved back of the chair, tube of antibiotic cream in hand. "No." She applied the cream on each wound, watching carefully what she was doing.

He'd had about all he could take. "Soon finished?"

She capped the tube and took bandages from her bag. "Soon."

She picked up his hand again to examine it, but this time his fingers curled around hers. "You have a healing touch." He could feel the same increase in the pulse at her wrist as he could feel at his temples. He stroked her pulse point with his index finger.

Her eyes were as dark blue as a deep sea. She pulled her hand away and in a husky voice said, "I have to apply the bandages." She did, her professional mode taking over. "Keep these on until you go to bed. Then apply more cream. Apply it three times a day. If the cuts bother you tomorrow, bandage them again. If you see any redness around them or swelling, come into the office immediately."

Clay respected the doctor in her. Although he knew he was playing with fire, he wanted the woman back instead. "Are you ready for that canoe ride?"

She put away the supplies and clicked the bag shut, looking indecisive. Finally, she answered, "I'd like that. But what about the games?"

Clay flipped the tablet toward him and skimmed down the list. "It looks good to me. We can worry about logistics and supplies closer to the time."

Canoeing on the lake an hour later, Paige thought about Clay's words "closer to the time." She'd probably be leaving a few weeks after the celebration. The thought created a melancholy she didn't understand. She also didn't understand all the feelings that had surged through her when she was caring for Clay's hand. She touched her patients automatically to give comfort . . . because she didn't know the language or because often she couldn't find the words. But with Clay . . .

He'd become much more than a patient. That's why she'd hesitated about the canoe ride. If she was going to be leaving in July, she shouldn't get involved. Should she?

Clay tapped her shoulder with the tip of his oar. "You're supposed to be relaxing, not thinking."

A few sprinkles of water dribbled down her arm. "I am."

"Don't fib to me, Dr. Conrad. You haven't pushed with that paddle in at least five minutes."

She swung her legs around until she sat facing him. He looked at home here. Big and strong, his muscles rippling under his green knit shirt as he rowed. His jeans stretched across his thighs as he braced his feet in the bottom of the canoe. The sun cast blue highlights in his black hair and a few strands of gray glimmered.

If they'd been sitting the opposite way with him leading, *she* could have watched *him*.

"You did that like a pro," he commented.

"I've been in canoes before. And on rubber rafts. That's how we traveled around some of the settlements."

He grinned. "And you're afraid to take a balloon ride?"

She smiled back. "Something about water seems safer than air."

Clay's gaze said her logic escaped him. He gestured at the blue lake water, the maples, evergreens, and poplars rising from the shore to the brilliant turquoise sky. The sun cast its rays, making diamonds dance on the water. "I think this is the most beautiful country I've ever seen. How does what you've seen compare?"

She laid her oar alongside of her leg and studied her surroundings. "This has a . . . civilized look. Maybe because I know just beyond are highways and developments and hospitals. The country I've seen is more primitive, not defined by man's hand. Except in the well-populated areas."

"No man-made lakes?"

"Only where the people were taught how to build reservoirs and irrigate the land. The problem is there aren't enough teachers and there's too much government red tape." She sighed, took a deep breath of air fragrant with pine, and smiled. "But I don't want to think about that now. This is so peaceful. It's just what I needed."

Clay laid his oar across his knees and pointed along the shore. "Look."

A mother duck and three ducklings swam close to the land. Every so often, one would plunge its head into the water, then look up, shaking off the excess. Paige laughed. "They make you want to go swimming."

"The lake water's still cold. Mid-July it warms up."

Her humor faded. She might be gone by then.

Clay dug into his back pocket and pulled out two small packets. "Peanuts. Want a pack?"

When she nodded, he tossed one to her. She caught the packet with both hands and placed it on her thigh unopened. "There's something I need to talk to you about." She hated to interfere with the pleasantness of their surroundings, the lovely time she'd had today. But she had to talk to Clay about Ben. Maybe she was being so persistent because she sensed Clay needed to talk to the teenager as much as the teenager needed to talk to him. As cautious as Clay was, she guessed deep pain was involved in what had happened to him—emotional and physical pain. The best way to deal with pain was to get it out in the open.

Clay opened his peanuts and popped a few into his mouth. "About our plans for the Fourth?"

"No. About Ben Hockensmith."

Clay poured out a few more peanuts then transferred them to his mouth. After he chewed and swallowed, he said, "I thought that was settled."

"I was afraid it wasn't. And I was right. Ben's session with the counselor didn't go well."

Clay carefully folded over the top of the packet and

stuffed them back in his pocket. "I hope you're not basing the success or, failure of his therapy on one session."

Paige restlessly moved her feet and the canoe rocked. "Ben has had therapy before. The month he was in the rehab hospital, he saw a counselor every day. He's sick of it. Right now, he doesn't need talk therapy. He needs a role model, someone to give him direction, someone to show him there's a reason to wake up tomorrow."

"That's one big responsibility you want to heap on someone's shoulders."

"I just need someone to get him started. Clay, he's hurting." As soon as she said it, she felt Clay withdraw.

"I'm not the only person on the planet who can help this boy."

"You're the only one I know about."

The nerve worked in his jaw. "You don't even know what happened to me. You have no idea—"

"Tell me."

Her gentle request seemed to bring him pain. The lines on his face, the deep green of his eyes told her better than words. His words tore at her heart. "I'd like to."

She waited.

"But there's more involved than simply talking about my recovery."

"A few hours with Ben could make a difference to both of you."

Clay raked his hand through his hair in frustration and looked out over the lake. Paige was right; a few hours could make a difference. Then again, they might not. In the meantime, his life would get turned inside out.

"Can you promise me something?" Paige asked quietly.

He didn't look at her. "What?"

"That you'll give it serious thought."

Clay picked up his paddle and pushed it into the water.

FOUR

Clay opened the closet in his living room Tuesday night, reaching to the shelf above his coats to pull out a stack of books he'd bought but never read. Maybe he could concentrate on a spy thriller. He couldn't seem to concentrate on much else. He needed to forget the blue of Paige's eyes, her soft touch, her compassion for one of her patients.

A glint of gold far back on the shelf caught Clay's eye. He pulled the carton around the books and lifted it down. The trophies. He'd forgotten they were up there. Purposely?

His father had delivered them soon after Clay moved in, when the floors were still unfinished, a bed, a stereo, and a chair his only furniture. His dad had asked him not to sign the final papers on the store, to use his insurance settlement for something other than the "ramshackle" house and a "bankrupt" business. He'd tried to convince Clay again that he should stay in Reisterstown and become his partner.

But Clay had known deep in his soul that he needed a fresh start without someone else's expectations driving him. From what he'd understood from his mother and

Trish, the old Clay had won those trophies more for his father than for himself.

Clay cut off the thoughts, unwilling to dig up emotions that he'd put to rest. He had no desire to bring back the nightmares that had stopped only last year. But he couldn't stop wondering if Ben Hockensmith was having the same difficulty with his father that Clay had experienced. Ben had been a football star. Had his father pinned his hopes and dreams on him? Was Ben feeling the pressure to fulfill everybody else's expectations without having the chance to decide what *he* wanted?

Had his friends stuck by him? Why wouldn't they? Ben remembered who they were. Yet if his rehabilitation had slowed him down, taken him out of the mainstream, he might have been moving too slow for friends to want to stick around.

Clay examined a trophy carefully, as always seeking a sign of recognition, a sign that all the doctors and experts were wrong. But reality stepped in. The trophy in his hands had been earned by a boy, a young man Clay didn't know. There was nothing he could do about that.

But there was something he could do about Ben. He could give the boy a pep talk. He wouldn't have to reveal anything about the amnesia. If necessary, he could tell Ben about the rehabilitation he'd had to go through with his shoulder. Nothing intense. Nothing wrenching. Nothing that might bring the nightmares back.

He didn't know why he hadn't thought of this before. Maybe because the recovery from his shoulder injury had been so much simpler than the rest of his recovery. But it might work.

Later that evening, Clay answered a knock at his front door and couldn't have been more surprised. Paige stood there, smiling hesitantly.

Her pretty blue eyes, simply styled hair, and uncertain

expression twisted something inside him that was deep and hungry. "A little late for house calls, isn't it?" he teased.

"I had a few late appointments. I wanted to stop by to apologize."

"For what?"

"For trying to make you do something that might not be right for you. May I come in?"

Clay stepped back and with a quick glance made sure the closet door was shut. It was.

Paige walked into the living room and sat on the sofa. He tried to ignore the way she looked so at home in his surroundings. Her questions, her curiosity, her caring were as natural to her as her blue eyes. "Would you like a cup of coffee? I made a pot a little while ago."

"Sure." She started to get up.

"No. Stay there. I'll bring it in."

Paige studied Clay as he walked into the kitchen. His legs were so long, his shoulders so broad. And her stomach still fluttered every time he smiled. It was his quiet strength she admired most; she could feel it whenever she was around him.

Looking around the room, she tried to find out more about the man. He liked restful colors—blue and earth tones. He appreciated texture—tweed, wood, hand-thrown pottery, rough plaster. Apparently he didn't like clutter. A Native American sculpture, stoneware lamps, and copper ship bookends holding *David Copperfield*, *The Prophet*, and *Wildlife of Northern America* were the only items decorating the furniture.

What she didn't find struck her as much as what she did. There were no photographs. Nothing . . . personal. Her most precious possessions were the photograph of her parents and a small ceramic clown her best friend in boarding school had given her. As much as she traveled, wherever she traveled, those two mementos went with her.

Clay returned to the living room and handed her a mug of coffee. He took his to the chair instead of sitting on the sofa beside her. In a way, she was glad. When he was too close, she had problems thinking straight.

"Did you decorate the house yourself?"

"For the most part. Trish made a few suggestions."

Clay's voice always softened when he spoke of his sister. Obviously, she was special to him. "Do you have a picture of her?"

Clay didn't even glance around as if one might be located somewhere else. "No."

"Your family isn't big on pictures?"

He took a sip of coffee from his mug and gazed at her over its rim. "I don't need pictures sitting around. The ones I need are in my head."

That was an unusual answer. It was on the tip of her tongue to ask what those pictures were until Clay asked a question she hadn't expected.

"What's Ben Hockensmith's biggest problem?"

Apparently Clay had done some serious thinking. "His frustration and anger that he can't play football. He doesn't want to change his dreams."

Clay set his mug on the hearth in front of the fireplace. "And you really believe if I speak with him, it will help?"

Her heart sped up. "Yes."

The silence in the room was an anticipatory hush.

Clay's green eyes were as serious as Paige had ever seen them. "All right," he said, "I'll talk to him. But I'd like it to be on a casual basis. I don't want him to feel trapped with me."

Paige couldn't imagine anyone feeling trapped with Clay. "We could go to the lake on Sunday for a picnic and a swim."

"You think Ben will go for that?"

She took a few sips of coffee as she considered his question. "He's been cooped up too long. I can't see him turning down sunshine, fresh air, and . . ." She smiled. "Good company." She paused for a moment. "What changed your mind?"

Clay shrugged. "I found something that reminded me—" He picked up his coffee mug. "It doesn't matter."

"Thank you."

He seemed embarrassed. "No thanks necessary." He nodded to her mug. "More coffee?"

She enjoyed sitting here with Clay, but she also knew she shouldn't stay. She'd be flying away in a couple of months. "No. I'd better go. Doc will worry. I didn't tell him I was going to stop by."

Clay stood, too. "I guess he might."

They both knew it was a poor excuse. But Clay had his reasons for keeping his distance; she had hers.

He walked her to the door. When she glanced up at him to say good-bye, the words wouldn't come and she couldn't look away.

He raised his hand and gently smoothed his thumb along her cheek. "What makes you care so much?"

"My background, I guess."

He searched her face, the depths of her eyes, and then shook his head. His hand lightly tapped her heart. "No, I think it's what's in here."

She could feel the lingering warmth of his fingers where he'd touched her. She'd never wanted to feel a man's hand on her breast before. The boldness of her thoughts should have shocked her, but it didn't. Because Clay was awakening something wonderful inside her and she wanted to feel his touch. The longing was such an ache, her eyes pricked.

She still couldn't say good-bye, but she managed, "Good night, Clay. I'll call after I talk to Ben."

He nodded and she opened the door. Walking into the evening, she took in a cool breath of air, waiting for it to blow out fires that both frightened and excited her.

Clay glanced at Paige beside him as he drove to the teenager's house. For Paige and Ben's sake, Clay hoped the outing would go well. He reminded himself he was going to watch his step today. He'd been incredibly stupid the other night, touching her like that. He'd only meant to . . . Hell, it didn't matter what he'd meant. He'd seen the surprise passion flare in her eyes, and he'd experienced his own body respond all too vehemently.

His aim today was to give Ben Hockensmith a pep talk and stay unaffected by Paige. As easy as paddling a canoe . . . he hoped. He took another look at Paige. She wore red shorts and her legs were every bit as lovely as the rest of her—tanned, smooth, curvy, and long. He could see the outline of her swimsuit's scooped neck under her navy top. He wondered what the rest of it looked like. What the rest of *her* looked like. . . .

He shut off the thought and asked, "How's Ben's family reacting to the accident?"

"Better than Ben. His dad says he'll take a second mortgage on the house and send him to college anywhere he wants to go. His mom makes sure he does his exercises and encourages him to get out. He's an only child, so he has all their attention."

"Is his dad having a problem now that football is out of the picture?"

"I don't think so. He wants Ben to get on with his life."

Clay wished his own father had wanted that for him. But his situation and Ben's were entirely different. Ben's father didn't feel as if he'd lost a son.

Ben was waiting outside along the curb. Paige could see his mother standing inside the screen door. She waved as Ben made his way to Clay's Blazer.

Ben was quiet as they drove to the lake. Paige tried to draw him out, but his answers were monosyllabic. Clay could feel the teenager staring at him and probably wondering about him. Paige had told Ben that Clay had been in an accident, too.

They found a weather-worn table in a grove of trees. Clay carried the picnic basket to the table. With his cane, Ben's carrying ability was limited, but he managed the jug of lemonade and his rolled towel. Paige brought her duffel bag and Clay's and the blanket for the grassy beach. They left the cooler in the Blazer for the time being.

The late-afternoon sun shone in the cloudless azure sky. "How about a swim first?" Paige asked cheerfully.

Clay said, "It's up to Ben. That water's still cold."

"I'm not afraid of cold water," the teenager muttered.

That might be true, but Clay knew he was afraid of other things. He watched Ben's eyes dart around the swimmers on the grassy shore. Then Ben looked down at his leg still encased in his jeans. Clay imagined what the teenager was thinking.

Clay took the blanket from the picnic bench. "Let's go sun on the beach. We can play a card game until we decide if we want to get wet."

Ben seemed thankful for the reprieve.

Paige exchanged a look with Clay that said she appreciated his thoughtfulness. He didn't want her appreciation. He didn't want anything from her that would increase the attraction between them. Because it couldn't go anywhere.

They settled on the blanket. To combat the awkwardness of strangers getting to know each other, they concentrated on a game of gin rummy.

After three rounds, Clay wiped his brow. "I don't know about you two, but it's too hot to sit here with clothes on. Ready for that swim?"

When neither Ben nor Paige answered, Clay lifted his shirt over his head.

"Jeez! What happened to you?" Ben asked.

Paige's gaze didn't seem to be drawn as much to the long jagged scars around Clay's shoulder as to his chest. Her eyes on him made the eighty-degree temperature seem over a hundred.

"Climbing accident."

"Mountain climbing?"

"Rock climbing. Mt. Everest was never in my plans." So he'd been told.

"Jeez," Ben repeated. "Did a bear get you, too?"

Paige moved slightly and Clay knew she was going to cut off Ben's questions. But he shook his head at her. After all, this was what today was all about, wasn't it?

"No bear. Rocks. The safety gear was defective. I went over the shelf first and . . ." He shrugged. "The rest is history. The doctors tell me I'm lucky to be alive."

Ben just stared and shook his head. "My leg doesn't look anything like that. And you don't care if people see it?"

"It's me, Ben. I have a right to swim or work out or do whatever I want. Sure, people stare. But usually a few words of explanation stop that. I just say I was in an accident. That's enough." He'd learned people could accept physical disabilities much more easily than mental ones.

Paige was watching him more closely than Ben.

Clay stood and unbuckled his belt. "So, you ready to swim?"

He noticed that Paige's cheeks, already rosy from the heat, suddenly flushed redder. He followed her gaze to his hands. Hadn't she ever seen a man take off his shorts? He looked at her in surprise.

She quickly averted her gaze. "You two go ahead. I'll be in in a few minutes."

Clay frowned, but his attention was diverted as Ben stripped to his suit. The teenager glanced at his cane but didn't pick it up. When his eyes met Paige's, he mumbled, "I can manage without it."

Ben picked his way carefully as he and Clay walked down the grass beach around clumps of sunbathers. Ben was limping but seemed steady enough. He tentatively smiled at a group of teenage girls who'd come out of the water. They returned the smile.

Paige crossed her fingers for luck. So far, so good. Feeling self-conscious, she took off her blouse and shorts. She wasn't used to parading around in next to nothing in mixed company. Yes, she'd had swimming classes in boarding school—with all girls. In med school, she hadn't had time for sunning or swimming. In Africa, she'd kept herself covered most of the time because of the cultural taboos and the heat. When she'd traveled with her mother, water was a precious commodity meant for survival, not recreation.

But today the lake called, and Paige was in the mood to answer. As she approached the water, she saw Clay's head break the surface. After a quick look around, he dived under again, swimming along the rope that bordered deeper water.

As she made her way to the lake, she felt less self-conscious. Everyone else wore bathing suits much less modest than her navy maillot. At the edge of the water, she swished her foot back and forth. It *was* cold. She hoped Ben's muscles wouldn't cramp.

Wading into the water steadily but slowly, she let her body get used to the temperature change. Goose bumps broke out on her arms.

When she was in waist high, Clay popped up in front of her. He ran his hands over his face and shook his hair away from his eyes. Water droplets sprayed her and she shivered, but not from the cold water.

She'd seen plenty of naked men since she'd been practicing medicine. But they'd been patients. With Clay, when she'd glanced at his gray trunks, the stretchy material hugging and molding, she almost couldn't breathe.

His scars were wicked. But his bare chest and shoulders had held much more fascination for her. She'd never seen such a beautiful male physique. Drops of water caught here and there in chest hair and rolled down his bronze skin. There was one drop on his left cheekbone she'd love to taste. . . .

"Ben seems to be okay. He said he wanted to do a few laps."

Clay's words drew her attention to his mouth. A very

male, sensual mouth. Hers went dry. She swallowed. "I don't want him to get overtired."

"I'll keep an eye on him. Anything I should know?"

She walked forward to get deeper into the water and to keep from ogling Clay. "Stay close when he's ready to get out. The exertion might make his leg feel weaker, and in the cold water he won't notice it."

"Will do. I—"

Paige stepped forward and the stony floor dipped unexpectedly. She lost her footing.

Clay's arm went around her to steady her. She looked up and was caught by his green gaze. His arm around her, her breasts pressing against his chest, created an excitement so powerful she couldn't speak; she could hardly breathe. Her nipples hardened; her pulse raced. Her head swirled, and she knew the sensation had nothing to do with the cold water and hot sun.

Clay's fingers languidly caressed the small of her back, sending spirals of tingling feelings through her body. As if it were the most natural thing in the world to do, Paige swayed gently forward.

"I forgot to warn you about falling. . . ." Clay trailed off to a whisper as his eyes suddenly darkened to jade. Paige thought she would get lost in them as slowly, ever so slowly, his head bent closer and she lifted hers, ready for the touch of his lips.

FIVE

"Dr. Conrad, I'll race you to the post!" Ben called.

Clay and Paige sprang apart. Clay's hand lingered on her arm only long enough to make sure she was steady on her feet.

Finding her voice, Paige called back, "I'll be right there."

When she turned to Clay, his face was expressionless, his tone neutral. "I'm going to deeper water for a few minutes. I won't be long."

She felt as if she'd just stepped into *very* deep water. She nodded because she didn't know what to say. As Clay swam off, she waded toward Ben, still feeling too much heat in her cheeks, feeling as if she'd missed out on something important.

The teenager shaded his eyes against the sun. "Sorry about that. I called before I saw his arm around you."

She floated her hands through the water. "I almost fell into a hole. He caught me."

"Anything you say, Dr. Conrad." Ben's words belied his skeptical grin. Then he shrugged. "Ready to race?"

She needed to be immersed in the water to forget about Clay Reynolds, to work off the excess energy of the adren-

65

aline still pumping through her. "Yes. One post length. You call it."

Ben steadied himself on his feet, glanced at her to see if she was ready, then said, "Ready. Set. Go."

Paige stroked through the water steadily, but didn't swim full tilt. She and Ben were swimming neck and neck. They emerged from the water at the same time.

Ben's face was strained so she asked, "Why don't we get out for a while? We can play another game of cards before we eat."

He nodded and waded with her to shallower water. Before she knew it, Clay had unobtrusively come up on Ben's other side. He must have been watching.

Ben was fine until they left the waist-high water. As he walked without the water's buoyancy, his left leg gave way. Clay caught him.

The teenager swore and Paige ran for his cane. She snatched it up and ran back. Clay was propping Ben up.

Ben glared at the cane with disgust. The group of girls he'd nodded to earlier were openly staring. "See what I mean, Dr. Conrad? They're looking at me as if I have two heads."

"They're just wondering—"

He yelled at the group. "This isn't a damn circus. Mind your own business."

The girls looked shocked.

"Not exactly the way to make friends, Ben," Clay said quietly.

The teenager grabbed the cane and turned on him. "And what the hell would you know? Sure, maybe you tore up your shoulder once upon a time, but it's fine now. You have two strong legs that'll let you do whatever you want. You've got nothing to complain about. I do. I can't even get from the lake to the blanket on my own power."

"I still have problems with my shoulder, Ben. But I lift weights; I never stop strengthening it."

"But it doesn't affect your life! You didn't have to quit something you loved because of it, did you?"

Paige noticed quite a few onlookers were watching with interest. She clasped Ben's shoulder. "Let's go to the blanket and talk."

Ben's face flushed beet-red. "See? You don't like to be stared at anymore than I do. See what it's like?"

He limped toward the blanket. When Paige glanced at Clay, he looked grim. He looked as if *he* was in pain. Did his shoulder bother him that much? Had this whole idea been a monumental mistake?

Unsettled, she followed Ben and sat down on the blanket beside him. "This is the first time you've been swimming other than therapy, Ben," she said gently. "You overdid it a little, that's all."

"I used to be able to swim forty laps easy."

Clay folded himself down on the other side of Ben. "That's the first thing you have to change, Ben. Thinking about used-to-be's won't get you anywhere." His voice sounded strained, but Paige didn't think Ben noticed.

"What did you used to do? How's your life different?"

"I don't go rock climbing. I've changed my whole life around because of the accident. Things that used to be important before aren't now."

"It's not the same thing. I don't want to change anything. I want to be able to walk over to those girls and ask one out and have her say yes."

"How do you know she won't?"

"Not after that little performance. Jeez, they could all see I couldn't even stand on my own two feet! I used to be able to date anyone I wanted—"

"Grow up, Ben."

Paige's instinct to defend made her interrupt. "Clay—"

"He needs to hear this, Paige."

"What do I need to hear?"

"You've got your life, Ben. From what Paige tells me, you've got a family who's willing to do anything for you.

You're intelligent and young and capable, and you can be anything you set your mind to be. Okay, you can't play football. So pick something else you can be good at and do it instead of whining about what you can't do. Do you know how many people who are in accidents never walk again, who have serious internal injuries that shorten their lives, who have to relearn—'' Clay stopped. ''Think about it, Ben. Think about how lucky you are. Think about what you can still *do*, rather than what you can't do.''

Clay stood, slipped on his moccasins, and grabbed his clothes. ''I'll go get the cooler so we can eat.''

He dumped his clothes on the bench and headed for the Blazer. And he'd thought he could keep this afternoon uncomplicated. Instead it was like paddling a canoe, all right. In a hurricane. What the hell made him think he could pull this off? He wasn't in the habit of deluding himself. He prided himself on facing life straight on. Well, his initial reaction to having anything to do with Ben had been correct.

Clay pulled the cooler from the backseat of the Blazer and slammed the door with more vigor than necessary. The last seven years, his life had been peaceful and ordinary. Then one compassionate, pretty doctor sashays into town and . . . damn!

Maybe he shouldn't have been so hard on Ben. But Clay had the feeling that everyone up to now had treated the teenager with kid gloves. Clay's family and doctors had treated him that way, too, for a while. Until they realized he'd never get his memory back. Then he became an oddity, a stranger, and they didn't know how to treat him. Today with Ben on the beach, the stares from everyone around them . . .

Clay remembered standing on his parents' front porch with the woman he'd supposedly loved before the accident. She'd looked at him so strangely when he'd told her he might never remember his life before the accident.

She'd shaken her head, told him recuperation was one thing, but never remembering the two of them as a couple was another. She said he'd changed and now they didn't have anything in common.

Since Clay couldn't remember loving her, the pain of parting hadn't been intense. But the pain of rejection had been. Her reaction had been the same as the reaction of friends he'd supposedly had before the accident. They didn't want to make the effort to make friends with the different man Clay had become. Like his father, they wanted the old Clay. He couldn't pretend to be someone he wasn't.

And then, more recently, there had been Clare . . . *enough*. This was what Clay didn't want. The rehashing. The memories of struggle and, God forbid—the nightmares. He wouldn't let them terrorize him again. The best way to keep them at bay was to forget everything to do with the accident and his recovery.

When Clay got back to the picnic table, Paige looked upset. "Ben wants to go home."

"Running away won't help, Ben."

Ben gave him a glare that could have knocked a giant flat. "I'm not running anywhere. I'm tired. What's the point of sticking around here—"

"Dr. Conrad went to a lot of trouble to get this picnic together. The least you can do is eat the food she prepared."

"Clay, it's all right. The fried chicken will keep."

"Ben?" Clay's tone held challenge.

"All right. We'll eat. But forget the canoe ride."

Clay opened the cooler and started lifting out the containers of food. "It's forgotten."

They ate, but they didn't talk much except for "Please pass the potato salad." Clay tried and so did Paige, but Ben's sullenness was difficult to ignore.

Clay drove Ben home. After the teenager had gone inside and Clay drove toward Doc's, he asked Paige, "You think I handled him all wrong, don't you?"

"I don't know. I just don't want him to become isolated."

"He is isolated. Recovery's a lonely process because he has to do it on his own. Others can help, but they can't do it. He has to break out of his self-pitying haze. And he might need some plain talking for it to sink in."

"Did someone do that for you?"

"Trish. She was always there holding up a mirror, making me see the truth, telling me what I didn't want to hear."

"She sounds special."

"She is. Full of laughter and hope and honesty."

"Did your recovery take long?"

"Much longer than I would have liked." He'd considered himself healed when the nightmares ended.

"Longer than Ben?"

"Longer than Ben." He couldn't say how long without telling her more than his shoulder was involved.

"You hurt your shoulder when you wrestled Shep, didn't you?"

Clay pulled into Doc's driveway. "I jarred it."

"But we went canoeing—"

"If I don't use it, it gets stiff. I put ice on it that night. The next day it was fine."

She laid her hand on his arm. "Would you tell me if it wasn't?"

His blood heated up. He knew her touch was only meant to give comfort, but instead it sparked dormant fires. "I don't know."

She shook her head. "Macho attitude."

He laughed. "Run into that often?"

"More often than I'd like. It prevents me from helping."

He covered her hand with his. "Ah, Paige. Out to heal the world. The time isn't always right." His thumb caressed the top of her hand. He wanted to stroke more than her hand. He took his fingers from hers and leaned away.

Paige folded her hands in her lap. "This afternoon didn't go the way I'd planned it."

"Does it ever?"

She smiled. "Maybe not."

The lights of desire in her eyes told him she remembered their embrace in the lake. He did, too. Much too well. He'd almost kissed her. But getting involved would be sheer stupidity. They'd both get hurt. It was a good thing Ben had interrupted.

"Clay, no matter what happens with Ben, thanks for trying today." And before he knew what was happening, Paige leaned toward him. Her lips were warm on his cheek, as gentle as a butterfly's landing but as disturbing as the embrace in the lake.

She slid toward the door. Without another word, she opened it and climbed out. As she walked up the path to Doc's door, Clay put his fingers to the place her lips had kissed.

The cold. Freezing, insidious cold burned his face, his fingers. He moved, and his leg fell into nothingness. If he moved too much, he'd fall into nothingness. Somehow he knew.

His head pounded and he couldn't open his eyes. It hurt too much. Shouts. People yelling. A drone above him. Or was the sound connected to the pounding in his head?

His shoulder burned with a different fire than the rest of his body. When he moved it, slicing pain stabbed him over and over. He had to get away from it. He had to escape the cold. He tried to turn over, but he couldn't and he found himself falling . . . falling . . . falling . . .

Clay awoke, his sheets drenched in sweat, his throat parched and dry, probably from yelling for help. He was shaking all over. He reached for the spread and pulled it on top of the sheet. He was cold. So cold.

Dragging in pockets of air, he tried to slow his racing heart. And then he swore a string of epithets that didn't begin to describe his frustration.

Determination took hold. He would *not* let the nightmares start again. He would not cry out in terror and spend the rest of the night recovering from the panic.

This nightmare had been mild compared to most of them. But what had brought it on? Had Paige stirred it all up? Clay touched his cheek where the touch of her lips still remained. Or had it been Ben? That made more sense. The day with Ben, the remembrance of similar experiences brought the unconscious to the surface.

Clay raked his hand through his damp hair. Either way, he'd stay away from them both.

The next morning, Clay went to the garage for his car. When he reached for the front door, he saw the cooler on the floor in the back. He'd forgotten to take it inside last night.

As he lifted it, he saw something on the floor next to it. Paige's sweater. She'd had it slung over her arm when she got into the Blazer. She'd said she might need it for the canoe ride. Somehow, it must've gotten thrown in the back when they packed up.

Clay set the cooler on the seat and picked up the sweater. It was white, soft, and he could smell a slight floral scent. Without thinking, he brought it to his nose and inhaled. It smelled like Paige—sunshine, flowers, woman. His body responded.

Right, Reynolds. You're not going to see her again, remember?

He tossed the sweater back into the car as if it were a hot potato. Hadn't last night taught him anything? He'd spent a sleepless night, tossing and turning, trying to forget the nightmare, block out Paige's face, set aside Ben's recovery process.

But he couldn't just cut Paige off. He'd drop off the

sweater during her office hours. That way he could return it, explain how busy he was going to be for the next few weeks, and say a simple good-bye. They'd already planned the agenda of games for the Fourth of July; he could take care of the rest himself. She was off the hook.

That's what he'd tell her. And then he'd leave. As simple as paddling a canoe.

Clay surveyed the doctor's office and found chaos. A young mother held a crying baby; two redheaded boys about six years old fought over a small plastic army figure. The first boy grabbed it away. The other child punched him in the arm. A pregnant woman, very pregnant, looked as if she couldn't be more tired. Two elderly women were scowling and muttering to each other. No receptionist sat at the desk.

Clay looked around again, suspecting something was wrong. Doc didn't run his office like this and Clay guessed Paige wouldn't either. He went to find her.

Before he'd gotten a foot into the hall, one of the elderly women called, "Hey, mister. It's not your turn."

He called back, "I'm not a patient."

As he walked down the hall, he found three examining rooms empty. That was odd. He reached the fourth and was debating whether to wait a few minutes or knock when the door opened.

Paige saw him and jumped. "Lord, you scared me. What are you doing here?"

He lifted her sweater. "I came to return this. What's going on? The patients in the waiting room look ready to riot."

Paige closed the door to the examining room. "I can't get caught up. I had a house call first thing this morning. Mr. Hick's little girl had a fever of one hundred and four and I thought it would be better not to bring her to the office. Then when I got here a half hour late, I found a message on the machine. My nurse and my receptionist went to a bridal shower yesterday and both got sick on something they ate. It's been bedlam since. I haven't had a chance to call for temporary help.''

Clay rested his hand on the doorjamb above her head. ''So you're trying to do the job of three people.''

Paige only had to tip her head a little to meet his gaze. ''I'm used to working alone. It's not that. But everybody here is so impatient. They want help immediately.''

She sounded more exasperated than frustrated. ''Your patients in Ethiopia didn't?''

''They'd waited months for medical care. A few hours didn't matter.'' She took her sweater from Clay's arm. ''Thanks for returning this. But I've got to get moving. If you want to talk . . .''

''No. I don't. But I could help out for a while. What do you need?''

She studied him for a moment. ''You're sure?''

''I wouldn't have offered if I didn't want to help.''

She motioned for him to follow her. ''I'm not going to turn a gift horse away.'' She smiled over her shoulder. ''That didn't sound right. What's the expression?''

He marveled at how fast she moved, as if chased by the devil. He corrected the idiom for her. ''You won't look a gift horse in the mouth.''

''My way makes more sense.'' She swerved into her office and picked up a clipboard from her desk. ''Use a separate sheet for each patient. Find out who was here first, second, et cetera. Show them to the examining rooms. Take down their complaints. Be as specific as you can. If they don't want to tell you, don't push.''

''Anything else?''

She handed him the clipboard and hurried to the waiting room. ''Find out what medications they're on. I'll take the two boys next. The patient in room four is getting dressed. He'll be out in a few minutes.''

Paige introduced Clay to the patients in the waiting

room, said he'd be helping her, and told them she'd be with each one as soon as she could.

Clay watched the expressions on their faces. It was amazing what a bit of attention, a smile, and an explanation did to defuse impatience. He had to hand it to Paige; she was good with people. He remembered her care when he'd cut his hand and her concern about Ben, her attempts to draw him out. She was genuine and caring. No facade.

Clay took the patients to the examining rooms, then started taking the information Paige had requested. When he asked the pregnant woman her name, she smiled shyly. "Miriam Jacobs. Nothing's wrong with me. This is just a checkup. Dr. Conrad says I have to come in every week now. I'm due in five weeks."

Clay wrote her name on the paper attached to the clipboard. "No problems?"

"No, it's just . . . never mind."

He raised his head. "If you want to wait to tell Dr. Conrad—"

"It's not that. It's just . . . I don't *need* to come every week."

"I imagine Dr. Conrad thinks it's important you do."

Miriam's hands fluttered. "But I can't pay her, and she's done so much already."

"You should talk to her about this."

"I have. She's letting me do sewing for her for payment. Even for office visits, that's not enough."

Clay wondered if Paige was used to bartering for services. It seemed like a good idea to him. It would put everyone on a more equal footing. "Maybe for her it is."

Miriam shook her head. "I know what doctors get to deliver babies. Even if she delivers my baby at home, she should get paid."

"Dr. Conrad's going to deliver your baby at home?"

"Uh-huh, if everything's all right. But she told me she'll call the ambulance if something doesn't look right.

She made me get a blood test and another test. A sonogram?''

Clay knew all about sonograms, CT scans, MRIs. He'd had the full gamut at one time or another. None of them was inexpensive. ''If you follow what Dr. Conrad says, I'm sure you and the baby will be fine.''

''It's my first. I'm scared.''

''I would be, too.''

Miriam smiled.

Paige considered checking the waiting room to see if it had filled up again. The morning's calendar had been loaded with appointments. She didn't take time to peek in, but hurried to her next patient, wondering where Clay was.

The door to the second examining room stood partially open. What Paige saw stopped her in her tracks. Clay was lifting a two-year-old into the air. The baby gurgled, smiled, and reached for Clay's chin.

Clay laughed and set the child on the examining table. But the toddler reached out for Clay, wanting more attention.

The baby's mother said, ''He's been crabby for the past hour. I should have given him to you sooner.''

''He was just bored, weren't you, little guy?''

The child stuck his thumb in his mouth and smiled around it.

Paige knew Clay was a gentle man. It shouldn't surprise her that he'd be good with children. Had he ever been in love? Had he ever considered having a family? In some ways he seemed so alone. But he had a family. He had friends. Figuring him out was more difficult than putting together one of Doc's jigsaw puzzles.

Paige entered the room. Clay handed her the clipboard, poked the toddler's tummy, receiving a giggle in return, and closed the door behind him.

When Paige finished with her patients, it was well after

noon. She returned the charts to the files in her office and went to the reception area. Her last patient was paying Clay for the visit.

The man waved at Paige. "Thanks, Dr. Conrad. Hope I don't see you for a while."

"Take *all* the antibiotics," Paige warned.

The man looked sheepish. "I will this time."

After he left her office, Paige sat on the corner of the desk and said to Clay, "I thought you'd be gone. Don't you have a store to run?"

"I have two people on the floor this morning."

Paige smiled. "You managed the office well. Thinking of a second job?"

He smiled reluctantly. "No, thanks. There's a list of callbacks you have to make. Nothing urgent. Mostly appointments. I didn't want to mess with your system."

"I don't know how to thank you, Clay. Without your help, I'd still be backed up."

"No thanks necessary. Just a neighbor helping a neighbor."

Something was different about Clay today. He was keeping himself remote.

He stood. "I'd better let you return your calls."

He seemed to take up most of the waiting room. "You said there was nothing urgent. I have sandwiches in the refrigerator in my office. You're welcome to share them."

He checked his watch. "No. I have to get going." He was halfway across the waiting room when he turned around and asked, "Are you really going to deliver Miriam Jacobs's baby at home?" He sounded wary of the idea and surprised.

"Yes. Why?"

"Just seems risky to me when a hospital's so close."

Paige considered information about patients confidential. Ben was a different matter since, in a way, she was consulting with Clay. But Miriam . . . "There are reasons."

"Yeah, she told me she can't afford it. I'm sure people would chip in—"

"Miriam won't accept charity. She lets me treat her only because we're . . . trading services." Paige had had Miriam hem slacks, replace zippers, mend frayed pillowcases.

"She does sewing for you."

"You and she had quite a discussion."

"She seemed to need someone to talk to. Is her husband out of work?"

"Clay, I really can't discuss—"

"Wait a minute. Jacobs. I heard someone in the store talking about him running out on his wife." Clay shook his head. "I can't understand men like that."

She imagined Clay couldn't. From everything she'd seen of him, she realized he had a strong moral character. "I'll take good care of her, Clay. She's healthy. I see no signs of problems, though you never know. I won't hesitate to call an ambulance if she needs it. You wouldn't believe the conditions under which I've delivered babies."

"Dirt floors and grass shacks?"

She could picture it all too vividly. "Sometimes. With Miriam I can make sure conditions are sterile. I've taught her Lamaze exercises. She wants to have a natural delivery for the baby's sake and so she recovers faster." Paige took her stethoscope from around her neck and stuffed it in her coat pocket. "Did Ben call you?"

"No. Why? Did you tell him to?" Clay didn't seem pleased by the idea.

"No. But I thought he might after he thought about everything you said."

Clay frowned and a lock of his black hair fell lower on his forehead. "Maybe I said too much. Don't hope for miracles, Paige. He's troubled and I don't think I'm the one to help him."

She wanted to brush Clay's hair from his forehead and ease the creases from his brow. "I think you're just the one to help him. But only if you want to. Has something happened to make you want to back off again?"

"No." He hesitated for only a fraction of a second, but she noticed it.

"Then what's wrong?"

"You saw what happened Sunday. I might have made the situation worse."

She hopped off the desk, approached Clay, and instinctively touched his arm. "You did what you could."

His muscles tensed under her fingers. "Yes, and sometimes we can't do enough." He pulled back, away from her touch, saying, "I have to go. I hope your afternoon doesn't stampede you like the morning."

She smiled. "I'll handle it. Thanks again."

Clay looked as if he wanted to say something more, but he didn't. He turned, and with a last long look, left the office.

SIX

Clay had left Paige, fully intending not to see her again. But as he drove home from work at five-thirty and passed her office, he noticed six cars still parked in the small lot. He thought about her being snowed under again and he veered into the parking area.

When he entered the office, the situation was similar to the morning's. He searched for the closed examining room door and knocked.

Paige opened it slightly and before she saw him said, "I'll get to you as soon as I—Oh, Clay!"

This morning she'd been busy but not harried. Now her cheeks were flushed, her hair was mussed where she'd brushed it away from her forehead and face. She looked drained. "Clipboard in your office?"

"Clay, I can't ask you to—"

"You're not asking."

Her stomach growled.

He gazed at her steadily. "Did you eat lunch?"

She brushed stray strands of hair away from her cheek. "I didn't have time. After you left, the phone started ringing. Before I knew it, the waiting room was full again. How many are out there now?"

"Five. You finish with this one, I'll take care of settling the others."

"Clay?"

"Don't say it," he warned with a grin.

She smiled a thank-you instead.

Clay was waiting for her in the hall when she finished with her patient. He held out a napkin with half a turkey sandwich. "I'd have brought you the whole thing, but I knew you wouldn't take time for that. Take a few deep breaths and eat this."

She tried to hide a smile. "*I'm* the one who's supposed to be giving orders."

He cocked his head. "I don't see why you can't share the honor."

She laughed and took the sandwich from him.

"And don't gulp it down."

She saluted him smartly. "Yes, sir."

Clay and Paige worked as a team as they had in the morning. Finally, the office and reception area were empty. Clay watched Paige as she shrugged out of her lab coat, hung it in her office, and sat in her desk chair, jotting notes on a chart. He stood in the doorway without her noticing.

She'd brushed her hair away from her face and tucked it behind her ear. A few wisps strayed across her cheek. She looked tired.

After the nightmare, he'd sworn he wouldn't see her again. But he kept coming back. Why? Because she needed help? That was one reason, but there were others. Some better left alone. Sometimes she seemed so untouched, other times there was a world of sadness in her eyes. He wanted to wipe that away.

He should lighten up and so should she. What could chase nightmares away faster than good times? They could both use an afternoon of pure fun. They could forget about Ben and whatever else bogged them down and simply have an enjoyable afternoon.

The decision made, he tapped lightly on the doorjamb.

She looked up and smiled. "I have to write this down before I forget." She finished the paragraph of notes, then put down the pencil and leaned back in her chair. "You're sure you don't want a second job?"

He sat on the corner of her desk. "I don't need a second job. But I do need a break. Have you ever been to an amusement park?"

She flipped her shoes off under the desk. "No."

"After today, Dr. Conrad, you need to be amused. We could go Thursday. After your visit to the hospital, of course."

Her blue eyes held his, then she said softly, "I'd like that."

He'd planned simply to have a day of fun with her, but her gaze and voice turned his insides upside down. How could one woman pack such a punch?

It didn't matter. An amusement park was not designed for romantic interludes. They *would* have fun.

Paige's eyes widened as she walked beside Clay along the asphalt path into the amusement park. She'd been amazed by the variety of license plates in the parking lot. Tourists came from all over the United States. Most of them towed laughing children as they bubbled with excitement.

Clay insisted on paying her entrance fee. With a shrug of a shoulder, he said, "It was my suggestion."

Paige thought he'd never looked more handsome or sexy. He'd gotten his hair trimmed. Though still shaggy, it lay more sedately over his ears. She wondered if it was as soft as it looked, or if it was more coarse to the touch. His black T-shirt stretched over defined muscles. He'd told Ben he lifted weights. She could imagine the up-down motion, his muscles pumping, the sweat gleaming on his bronze skin. Her gaze dropped a bit lower.

His black shorts were beltless, the band flat against his

waist. She'd never seen a man his age in such beautiful condition. She remembered the way he'd looked in a bathing suit and her heart beat faster. Thoughts of Clay were becoming too prominent. This was just a day away from work, a day to have fun.

Clay cupped her elbow and led her to a giant Ferris wheel with cages as cars. "We'll start out easy."

"Really? What else do I have to look forward to?" Whenever he held her, no matter how casually, her heart skipped beats.

"The roller coaster."

"I've seen pictures of them, but I never rode one. Are you sure they're safe?"

He stopped and turned her toward him. "This from a woman who rides a raft through a jungle, lives for weeks in the desert? Dr. Conrad, I'm surprised you could think I'd lead you into danger."

His green eyes could lead her into a kind of danger she'd never known—the danger of losing her heart. She fought the idea away and smiled. "Danger's in the eye of the beholder."

He laughed. "There are two roller coasters. They're both perfectly safe. Then there's the ride that turns you upside down."

"I think I'll skip that one. The only ride I've ever been on is a carousel."

He grabbed her hand. "Then your experience has been sorely lacking. Let's get started."

The Ferris wheel *was* easy. The cable cars were a snap. The pirate ship that moved higher back and forth as it swayed made her a little seasick. The carousel gave her the thrill she remembered as a child, but an even bigger thrill because Clay was riding the lion beside her horse, his hair rumpled from the breeze, his large hands clasped around the pole. When he grinned at her, she didn't think any ride could be more exciting.

Then came the roller coaster—the monumental one on the wooden tracks.

Clay tried to encourage her. "It just *looks* intimidating."

She gazed at the steep hills, the low valleys, what seemed to be miles and miles of weaving track. "You're sure this is going to be fun."

"Absolutely." He looked up at the graying sky. "If it doesn't rain." He dropped his arm around her shoulders and guided her to the entrance. She felt safe and protected, and not even the size of the roller coaster could diminish that feeling with Clay's arm around her.

But once in the car, Clay's arm wasn't around her. She held on to the bar in front of her.

Clay tapped her knuckles. "Relax. Just go with the sensation."

Paige loosened her grip so her knuckles weren't white. But as soon as their car started forward, she tightened it again. *Go with it,* she told herself. *Go with it.*

The mantra lasted until they started to ascend the first steep hill. She shut her eyes.

Clay whispered in her ear. "You can't see with your eyes closed."

His breath on her lobe caused chills to break out on her arms. "What's there to see?" she squeaked, taking a peek.

"Look over there at the gardens, the brilliant colors. See the lake and . . ."

"Uh-oh. I think I want to get off." They'd almost reached the top of the hill.

Clay put his hand over hers. "Take a deep breath and—"

His words were lost in the screams and rush of air as they plunged over the top and down to a bottomless valley. At least it felt that way. Paige couldn't tell if the scream she'd heard was hers or someone else's.

She had no time to recover from the first swoop. They ascended a second incline and zoomed to earth again.

She'd just caught her breath when the car swerved around a sharp curve. She was thrown against Clay and as the car took another sharp drop, her arm went around his chest so she could hold on to something stable.

She felt his sharp intake of breath. She heard the pounding of his heart. The warm feel of him against her cheek was her ballast against the wild ride.

The car screeched to a slower speed then coasted to the end of the line. Neither of them moved. The thumping of his heart was louder. The heat emanating from under his shirt steamier. If she rubbed her cheek against him, what would he do?

She wasn't courageous enough to find out. Lifting her head, she found his lips only inches away. His green gaze mesmerized her, and suddenly she went on a second roller coaster ride that had nothing to do with the ride in the amusement park.

He cupped her chin in his hand and caressed her face. In a moment he'd . . .

"Miss. Mister. We're loadin' up."

A teenager stood beside the track, waiting to unhitch the safety bar so they could disembark. A long line of patrons waited to climb into the cars.

Paige broke away from Clay and knew she was turning at least three shades of red. "Sorry." She didn't glance at Clay, but stepped out and hurried down the ramp. She didn't stop until she reached the main thoroughfare.

When she stopped, Clay was close behind her. He asked casually, "Was it worth the thrill?"

He was talking about the roller coaster ride, but what she remembered was his hand on her cheek. "I'd try it again sometime." She was curious, intrigued, excited that Clay's touch could create the same sensations as a roller coaster. Had he felt anything as he held her? She wasn't brave enough to ask.

What if he kissed her? Then what? She'd be leaving;

he'd be staying. Then again, what harm could one kiss do?

They went to the shows at the park between trying the rides. Paige was especially aware of Clay's nearness. He seemed careful not to touch her again. She wondered what was going through his head as they watched the performers sing and dance. The entertainment was professional, but her mind was on Clay.

The show-tune review over, they stepped out of the building. The sky was a more sullen gray. Dark clouds skittered by, blown by a breeze that hadn't been evident before.

Clay said, "A thunderstorm's brewing. Do you want to take a chance and get something to eat or leave now?"

"Let's get something to eat." She didn't particularly want the day to end. This having fun could be addictive, especially when she was having fun with Clay.

The lines of tourists had thinned so they didn't have to wait long for their food at the streetside restaurant. Clay carried their plates of burgers and fries to a table with an umbrella. Paige set down the drinks and napkins. But as soon as she did, the wind picked up the napkins, tossing them to the asphalt, then sending them across the street.

Clay waited until Paige sat before he took his seat. "We'd better eat fast if we don't want to get wet."

Paige took a bite from her hamburger. "Do you come here often?"

"Two or three times a season."

Her curiosity got the best of her. "Who with?"

"Trish and I usually come once. Friends other times."

That didn't tell her what she wanted to know. "Do you date much?"

He popped a few fries into his mouth. "Now and then."

She didn't swear. If she did, now would be the time. "No one can evade questions better than you."

"What do you want to know, Paige? Should I give you a list of women I've seen in the last six months?"

"Do you have one?"

He was stone silent for a moment, then he laughed and tweaked the end of her nose. "For a minute there, I thought you were serious."

She wasn't sure if she was or not. "I just wondered if there was anyone . . . special."

The wind whipped up the side of Clay's plate. He held it with one hand, picked up his burger with the other, and didn't meet her gaze. "There's no one special."

His voice was rough as if the admission was difficult, and she knew she'd better drop the subject. Their close contact on the roller coaster had ended their ability to have comfortable conversation. Now everything seemed to be a land mine.

Large drops of rain plopped on the umbrella and the pavement. Clay stood. "Do you want to get stuck in a gift shop or make a run for the car?"

"Let's go to the car. We don't know how long it will last."

They dumped their plates and cups and hurried toward the exit. When they'd walked from the lot to the entrance, it hadn't seemed so far. Now with the drizzle and wind, the car was in no-man's-land. Halfway across the parking lot, the rain came down in earnest. It pelted Paige's face and molded her blouse to her body. By the time Clay unlocked the passenger side of the Blazer and opened the door for her, she was drenched.

She climbed in and unlocked his side. He slid in with a rush and slammed the door. He rested his arms on the steering wheel then looked over at her. "Think we made the wrong choice?"

She laughed—a free laugh that floated around the inside of the car. Clay joined in.

She wiped laugh tears away from her eyes and pushed her wet hair behind her ears . . . and shivered.

Clay must have seen it because he turned in his seat and fished on the floor in the back for something. He lifted a black flannel jacket and handed it to her. "Wipe off with this and put it around your shoulders." He flipped on the ignition. "I'll turn on the heater."

"You're wet, too."

He jabbed the buttons on the dashboard. "I'll dry."

She shook the sleeve of the jacket at him. "It'll be over an hour until we get home."

"I'm fine."

That macho attitude again. Taking the soft cuff in her hand, she leaned toward him. He didn't move.

She dabbed his forehead, his cheekbones, but when her ministrations slipped to his neck, he grabbed her wrist. "Enough, Paige."

It was a warning, but she felt reckless. She ran the material from his chin to his shirt collar. He closed his eyes and said sharply, "Paige . . ."

It was more than a warning this time. She dropped her hand into her lap. "I don't want you to catch a cold."

"As hot as I am at this moment, that could never happen."

She wasn't exactly sure what he meant and she wanted to find out. "The rain should have cooled you off."

"I'm talking about *you*, not the weather. Each time you touch me . . ." He swore. "We've got to get home."

He put the car in reverse and backed out of the parking place. After a few miles, he switched on the radio and she knew he didn't want to talk. She put the jacket around her shoulders, breathing in Clay's scent, rested her head against the seat, and tried not to think.

The storm became more severe the farther they drove. Paige could hardly see through the windshield and could imagine the difficulty Clay was having. But he didn't pull over. They traveled slowly but surely.

Eventually, he turned onto the road leading to Doc's. Suddenly Clay screeched to a halt.

He swore when she braced her hands on the dashboard, then murmured, "Sorry."

She caught her breath and asked, "What's wrong?"

Clay motioned through the windshield. "There's a tree across the road. They must have had a worse storm here. We'll have to go to my place and get dried off until it's cleared."

He didn't sound happy about it.

When they arrived at Clay's, they ran immediately to the house. Inside, Paige shook off Clay's jacket. "Now it's wet, too."

"It doesn't matter." He motioned to the upstairs. "Go on. Take a hot shower so you don't get sick. There's a robe on the inside of the door. Drop your clothes outside and I'll throw them in the dryer."

"I should call Doc."

All business and practicality, Clay said, "I'll call him and tell him what's going on. He can let me know when they clear the road."

Trying to stop shivering, Paige went straight to the upstairs bathroom, undressed, and dropped her clothes outside the bathroom door. It felt strange to have someone taking care of her. She'd been on her own most of her life. Even when she'd been with her parents, they'd expected her to take care of herself. And she had. Proudly. But Clay's caring about her felt . . . nice.

The hot shower warmed her to her bones. After she toweled off, she reached for Clay's robe. It fell to her feet. She wound the belt around her waist twice, feeling as if she were wrapped up in an oversized velour blanket.

She found a blow dryer under the sink and used her fingers to push her hair into order. Without a brush, the result was a fluffy brown mass framing her face. Coming out of the upstairs bathroom, she passed Clay's bedroom and couldn't help peeking in. The four-poster pine bed looked king-size. It would have to be for Clay to be comfortable. The room had stark white walls broken only by the forest-green-and-navy-patterned drapes and bedspread.

It was a masculine room. A picture of herself and Clay intertwined on the bed flashed before her eyes.

Paige quickly went downstairs. Shep lay in front of the fireplace as if he expected Clay to start a fire any time. Paige smiled until she stood in the doorway to the kitchen and saw Clay.

He was making a pot of coffee and his back was to her. He'd changed into a clean T-shirt and jeans. His hair was still damp but looked as if he'd taken a comb through it.

He heard her when she moved toward him. Turning, he gestured to the table. "There's a pair of socks if you want to—"

His eyes slowly ventured from her fluffy hair to her bare toes. His eyes darkened and seemed to burn into her.

She took a few more steps. "Did you call Doc?" Her mouth was dry and the words came out in a bumpy cadence.

"Yes. He was glad to know you were safe." Clay's voice was husky.

"Of course I'm safe. I'm with you."

At that, Clay shook his head. "Paige, do you know how absolutely enchanting you are?" He reached for the lapel of his robe and straightened it carefully.

She cleared her throat. "It's a little big."

He slid his fingers through her hair, brushing it away from her face. "I've been trying not to touch you."

She wished he'd run his fingers through her hair again; it felt so good. But she tried to concentrate on their conversation. "Why?"

"Because I know I shouldn't kiss you."

Her throat tightened. "Would it be so terrible?"

He exhaled a huge sigh. "No."

"Clay . . ."

"When you look at me like that—" He tilted her head up and bent his.

SEVEN

The touch of Paige's lips broke Clay's control. His arms slipped from her face to her back and pulled her closer. Her kiss was tentative, and for a moment he thought about stopping. Then she sighed and the idea of his tongue touching hers swept restraint to a back corner of his mind.

When she raised her arms and threaded her fingers through his hair, he thrust into her mouth, demanding she respond. Her tongue slid over his, then danced around it, inciting fires he'd thought would never burn again.

The inside of her mouth was seductive satin, the taste of her was as sweet as summer-ripe fruit, the feel of her in his arms created loneliness so deep, he sought to assuage it any way he could.

He'd intended to kiss her once, lightly, and let her go. Yes, it would have teased him. But he knew his own boundaries. He could tell when easy desire escalated into hungry passion. And he knew he could stop before the passion took over.

Before he could have stopped. Before Paige. As her tongue feverishly stroked his, the desire flared into passion, and then blazed into a ferocious elemental need. Clay lowered his hands to her waist, and as their bodies met, even with the barrier of clothes, the universe exploded. Paige's response changed, becoming almost frantic. Her fingers massaged his scalp and caressed his neck as she arched toward him. Could she possibly know what she was doing to him?

The world tilted. Reality went berserk. His mind spun as fast as all his senses. He was caught between needing and knowing he shouldn't. There was a threshold he shouldn't cross—one that led to intimacy and truth and heartache.

Clay knew he'd shut off this kind of passion. He'd shut off the hunger and yearning in order to make himself an emotionally comfortable life. Paige had wiped the comfort away. She'd shaken up his space and he was still trying to put a lid on the effects. So what the hell was he doing kissing her?

The kiss was more than it should have been, less than he wished it could be. Red-hot need laced his body until the desire surging through him aroused him to a height he'd never experienced. What about Paige reached down inside him, took hold, and wouldn't let go? She was just a woman.

Just a woman? No. A special woman. Too vulnerable. Too caring. Too . . . dangerous. He could lose the simplicity he held on to with both hands. He could lose himself. He couldn't take that chance.

He ended the kiss and lowered his arms. If he kept holding her, he'd want to hold her forever. Control wasn't so hard to maintain. Physical distance led to emotional distance.

Paige's expression was bemused. His robe gaped at her breasts and the creamy flesh made his fingers itch. He longed to touch her. He backed up. Physical distance was all he needed.

"Clay?"

"What?" He regretted the sharpness of the question,

but he couldn't be tender now, not if he was to keep from kissing her again.

"Tell me how you feel."

So honest. How could he be just as honest and not hurt her? "I'm sorry I let that happen."

She looked deflated, disappointed. "I see."

No, she didn't, but this is the way it had to be. "Your clothes should be dry by now. I'll get them." He started toward the basement door, trying to still his shaking hands.

"Would you like me to start a fire in the fireplace?" Paige asked tentatively.

A fire, shadows, warmth, flames flickering on Paige's face. Talk about temptation. His first thought was *no way*. But then he looked at her bare feet, her arms wrapped around her as if she was cold. Maybe the hot shower hadn't taken away her chill.

"That's fine. There's kindling in the box behind the sofa."

She nodded.

Clay opened the door to the basement. She was one capable lady. One kiss wouldn't throw her off balance for long. As he descended the steps, he told himself that's what he believed.

Two days later, Paige was cooking supper when the telephone rang. She looked at it expectantly, hoping the caller would be Clay. She hadn't heard from him since he'd brought her home after the storm. Soon after she'd started the fire, Doc had called, saying the township office had sent men to remove the tree blocking the road.

The time she'd spent with Clay after the kiss had been awkward and stilted. She blamed her inexperience with men for believing the kiss had affected Clay as much as it had her. She'd felt excitement from the top of her head to her toenails. Her breasts had tingled and she'd wanted to press them against Clay. She relived the moments when his desire was hard against her. Her own deep, dark arousal had astounded her.

Somehow in the midst of all that, she'd known Clay possessed a strength she needed and that her feelings for him went deeper than she ever could have imagined.

But then he'd said . . .

She picked up the receiver, hoping to hear his voice. But it was her mother's voice she heard instead. "Paige, are you there?"

"Yes, Mom."

"I'm not having much success getting volunteers long distance. So I'm coming to the States for two weeks."

Paige's stomach lurched.

"There are a few doctors I want to speak with in Los Angeles," her mother went on. "They might be interested in working here for six months or a year. I'm also going to give presentations to classes of residents. Maybe I can wake up their social consciousness."

"You're flying just to Los Angeles?"

"Oh, no. Texas and Ohio, too. Then I thought I'd end up in Langley and we could fly back together."

Paige's heart skipped a beat. "When will that be?"

"Around the beginning of July. I can't give you exact dates because I'm going to mine the wealth wherever I find interested doctors."

"I might not be able to fly back with you. If Doc's not fully recovered—"

"Is he there? I'd like to talk with him."

"No, he's not. He drove to a friend's in Baltimore."

"It sounds like he's getting around just fine."

Paige could see improvement in Doc day by day. He was getting out more, visiting, walking. Just yesterday he'd started back at the office on a part-time basis. But she didn't want to push him. "He's recuperating nicely. But I don't know if he's ready for a full-time practice yet."

"Of course, I understand that. But you know, Paige, at

his age and in his condition, with the blockage fixed, he's in better shape than he was before the open-heart surgery."

Her mother, like always, was pushing to get what she wanted—Doc back in practice, her daughter by her side. Paige thought she'd at least have until the end of July to put her life in perspective. But it didn't look that way now.

"Mother, we have to talk."

"Yes, I know we do. We have plans to make. I've outlined our options for the next year and sent them to you. When I get to Langley, we can discuss them. I miss you. It's not the same without you here."

"Mom, the reason I left. I'm not sure I've resolved—"

"We'll talk about it when I get there. You just think of this time as a long vacation. I really have to go. You take care. I'll be in touch."

Paige hung up the phone, wondering if her mother was right. Was this just a long vacation? It didn't feel like a vacation when she was seeing patients. She thought about canoeing on the lake, the day at the amusement park. She supposed those activities would classify as vacation-like. But Clay and Doc seemed to think those things should be part of everyday living.

Who was right? Her mother, striving to heal anyone who didn't have adequate care? Doc, healing patients in his own environment? Clay, working and living and playing to get the most out of life?

Was one way better than another? Couldn't they somehow be combined?

Her mother was counting on Paige to return to Africa with her. Could Paige even contemplate disappointing her?

Trish's blond curls bounced around her face as she tried to pull the ball from Shep's mouth.

"Let it go and he'll drop it right in front of you," Clay suggested.

"You've got to be kidding."

Clay continued to thin out the rows of carrots in his garden. "Nope. It's his latest idea of a game. Just stand up and act as if you could care less."

Trish wiped her hands on her jeans and stood as tall as her five-foot-four frame would let her. "So . . . are you going to come to Reisterstown next Saturday and go with Michael and Dad to get measured for your tux?"

"Can't I just give you my measurements?"

"I want your opinion."

He took a long look at her hopeful face. "Trish, you know you're asking for trouble if you expect me and Dad to agree."

Shep dropped the ball in front of her. She picked it up and tossed it as far as she could across the yard. "Maybe you'll both pick the same one."

"Maybe Michael should make the choice and we'll go along with whatever he wants."

"Clay, I know Dad can be difficult, but I think he's going to try to be agreeable."

"As long as you agree with him. As long as I agree with him."

"It still hurts, doesn't it?"

Clay glanced down at the garden, stalling before responding. The crop was going to be good this year. With adequate rain, he'd have fresh vegetables all summer. "I don't know what you're talking about," he finally answered.

"It still hurts that you can't get close to Dad."

Clay's chest tightened and he forgot the garden and felt the pain. His father had been involved in his therapy until he realized Clay would not regain his memory. Then he'd bowed out of the picture as if he was just waiting for the impossible to happen. But that was the problem. Regaining lost memories was impossible in Clay's case. He had experienced joy each day in new accomplishments. But only his mother and Trish had shared them.

It shouldn't matter, but it did.

Shep came running back to Trish and dropped the ball at her feet. "Talk to me, Clay. You've been quiet since I got here. What's going on?"

It would be so easy to deny something was going on. But this was Trish. "I met a woman. Or rather she met me. And my life hasn't been the same since she drove down the lane." He told Trish about Ben and about Paige's requests for his assistance. He recapped the past few weeks' events, and ended by telling her about the nightmare.

"How do you feel about her?"

Paige had the ability to reach deep inside him, and he felt alive when she was near. Her wonder on the amusement park rides, her childlike pleasure at things he took for granted, like cotton candy and chocolate kisses, made him feel he was recapturing the years he'd lost. He believed his life would be so much fuller with her in it and the loneliness would fade away. But then he faced reality. "I don't want to feel anything."

"But you do."

"Too much," he muttered. So much sometimes it tore him up inside. Especially when he kissed her.

"Would the problem be solved by going to bed with her?"

Leave it to Trish to cut to the core. With Paige, he could never use the term "going to bed," or "sleeping together," or any of the other euphemisms. If he kissed her, if he touched her the way he wanted, if he buried himself inside her, they'd be making love. And he suspected the experience would be earth-shattering. But that he couldn't share with his sister.

Instead he said simply, "I think that would cause even greater problems."

"So this is more than attraction?"

"It's attraction on too many levels."

"It's easier for you since she's leaving, isn't it?"

"Easier?"

"Sure. If you wait it out, she'll be gone and you won't have to tell her anything."

Clay scowled, but he couldn't intimidate Trish or divert her questions.

"Would the risk be so terrible? From what you've just told me about her, she sounds understanding."

He straightened and rubbed his shoulder. "I don't want her pity."

"Understanding and pity aren't the same, Clay."

"If I tell her about the amnesia, nothing will be the same."

"If you don't tell her, you'll never know what you could have had."

"You don't understand."

Trish walked over to the edge of the garden so she could look at her brother without squinting into the sun. "Yes, I do. You feel as if you have a friendship with her now and you're afraid you'll lose that."

He had a little bit of everything with Paige—friendship, respect, desire. Yet he really had nothing at all. "It's more complicated than that."

Trish stuffed her hands into her back pockets. "Just remember—nothing ventured, nothing gained."

He'd ventured plenty of times and gotten hurt. Until he'd wised up. "I still remember Clare's reaction, her shock at the nightmares."

"They took her by surprise because you hadn't told her, either."

"But once I did . . . I can still remember her expression when I told her I had to memorize the photo album because the pictures really meant nothing."

"It's not fair to put all women in the same category. You're playing it too safe. Clare's the only person in Langley you ever told about the amnesia."

He hadn't even told Doc. Doc knew about the accident, about the head injury, about Clay's learning to read and write again, but Clay had never told the physician he'd lost the first twenty-five years of his life. He thought about what Trish had said. Playing it safe kept him from getting hurt.

He looked at his sister and tried to explain. "I'm accepted here, Trish. Luckily Clare left town soon after our break-up or more people would know. It's hard to keep a confidence that is that . . . strange. So why tell anyone? Why would I want to put into jeopardy the camaraderie I've established and the friendships I've made?"

"To find something even better. You know, Michael asked me to marry him three times over the past year. The first two times I was afraid to say yes. I was afraid our relationship would change if I did. Well, it has changed. It's changed for the better. Fear could have robbed me of something very special."

She came over and knelt down beside him. "Did you do this row yet?"

He observed her manicured fingernails, polished in pink. "No. But you don't have to help to get me to Reisterstown. I'll be there if you want me there."

She smiled. "I know you will." She fished in his box of garden tools until she unearthed an old pair of gloves. "I need to learn how to garden. We're thinking about putting a contract on a house, and I'd like to have a garden. You can teach me everything I need to know."

Yes, he could teach her about growing a garden, but she always taught him about life. It didn't seem a fair trade.

Clay closed up Doc's storage shed Monday evening, all the while aware Paige was inside the house. At least he presumed she was; her car was sitting in the driveway. They hadn't spoken since the night he'd kissed her.

Doc's truck wasn't in the garage, so Clay assumed Paige was alone. He *could* leave.

But he remembered the hurt in her eyes when he'd

answered her question about the kiss. It had lingered in their blue depths when he'd driven her home.

He went around to the front door and knocked. No one answered. Clay called softly through the screen door. "Paige?"

He tried the latch and found it unlocked. Going through the living room, he stopped in the doorway to the kitchen.

Paige was seated at the table, reading what looked like a letter. An envelope lay torn open in front of her. She hadn't heard him come in and he didn't want to startle her. So he said again softly, "Paige?"

She lifted her head, and he saw tears glistening in her eyes.

He didn't think about whether he should or shouldn't go to her. He crossed the dining area and stood close to her chair. "What's wrong?"

She shook her head and attempted to keep her lower lip from trembling by biting it.

He clasped her shoulder. "Has something happened to your mother?" He couldn't imagine what else would cause her this turmoil.

She made an effort at composure and managed to stop her lip from quivering. "No. It's me. I don't know what I want to do, what I'm going to do, what I should do."

He pulled out a chair and swung it close to hers. When he sat, his leg brushed hers, but he didn't move it away. "What's in the letter?"

Paige ran her finger down a list. "Mother drew up a schedule for the next six months."

"New places?"

"We've been at some of them before. I just don't know if I can go back. The reason I left . . ."

Her voice broke and he took her hand. It seemed the most natural thing in the world to hold it and give her comfort. "Tell me why you left."

Her eyes filled with tears she couldn't blink away. She tried but then she let them come. "I lost a child."

Emotions crashed through Clay—compassion, sorrow, jealousy, astonishment. "You were pregnant?"

She shook her head and brushed her hand across her cheek. "No. It was one of the village children. I'd been treating her for two weeks and I thought she might be one of the lucky ones. But . . . she wasn't." Paige took a deep breath and wiped the tears from her other cheek.

Clay could see how upset she still was about the loss. It was as if she'd lost a child of her own. "Was this one special?"

Paige looked at him with such anguish that he wanted to take her in his arms and hold her until it all went away. She said haltingly, "They're *all* special. Mother says I get too personally involved, that I have to learn to stay detached. I tried. But I couldn't. This child, Clay, she was just one too many. I completely lost it. I couldn't stop crying. That's when I knew I'd been there too long and seen too much."

Now he understood. He understood her sadness and uncertainty. "So you came here to help Doc."

"That's what I told myself, that's what I told my mother. But I came here to escape for a while."

"Treating Doc's patients is an escape? A vacation to Hawaii is an escape." He squeezed her hand. "You're doing worthwhile work here, too. Paige, you can't go back before you're ready. You'll only hurt yourself and not help anyone."

She made a fluttering gesture with her hand. "But will I ever be ready? Don't you see, Clay? The longer I stay away, the harder it will be to go back."

He rubbed his thumb back and forth over the top of her hand, trying to soothe her, trying to give her something she needed. "That tells me you don't want to go back."

"I *do.*"

"You can heal here."

Her eyes were huge blue pools. "It's not the same."

"Why?"

"People in the States have access to care. There are thousands of doctors here."

Clay slipped his thumb over one of her knuckles and then another. "What about Miriam?"

"What about her?"

"Would all doctors treat her? Would they deliver her baby at home?"

Paige closed her eyes for a moment. "But she's only one."

"One matters, Paige. And what about Ben? His problems are as real as unsterile conditions. The problems here are different, but they aren't any less important. You have to consider what's best for you *and* your patients."

She opened her eyes and stared at the wall ahead of her. "All my life I've wanted to follow in my mother and father's footsteps. I wanted to work beside them. I want them to be proud of me."

"How could they not be?"

She shrugged and gave him a sidelong glance. "I was away from them so much growing up. So when I was with them, every moment counted. I wanted . . . oh, I can't explain it."

But he could. "You wanted the approval and love you couldn't feel when you were miles apart."

She looked at him directly. "Yes, but also what I did had to be special. I had to succeed. Don't you see? Not going back would be admitting I failed."

Paige was being torn apart by her parents' dream and her knowledge that that dream might not work for her. "Is it so wrong to want a different life from your parents'?" he asked.

She shifted restlessly on her chair, her leg lodging closer to his. "I don't know. But I have to make up my mind soon. My mother's coming to Langley the beginning of July."

The beginning of July. She'd originally said two

months. Now it was even less. "There's something else you might want to consider."

"What?"

"Is your mother's pride in what you do more important than your happiness?"

Her voice was a whisper. "That's the problem. I don't know."

Paige needed time to try out the "normal" life she'd never had. But it seemed time was the one thing she didn't have.

He couldn't give her the time she wouldn't give herself, he couldn't give her the solution to her problems, but he could give her comfort and the understanding she needed to work her dilemma through.

He turned her hand over and tenderly stroked her palm. "Whenever you need to talk, I'll listen."

She gave him a brave attempt at a smile. It was the bravery that made him lean forward to touch his lips to her forehead and give her a hug. That's all he'd intended to do. But the intention slipped by the wayside.

The fragrance of her hair caught him. The softness of her skin under his lips ensnared him. Her pliant response when her arms wrapped around his back to return the hug led him to her lips. She kissed as she did everything else—wholeheartedly, with all her being.

When he slid his tongue through her lips, only the first touch of her tongue was tentative. Then all hesitancy vanished as she tasted him as much as he tasted her. He wanted to get closer, feel more of her, but couldn't because of their positions on the chairs.

He stood and pulled her up with him, but the movement broke the intensity and Paige backed away.

Her eyes glistened again, but her voice was strong. "You said you didn't want this to happen. You said—"

She was thinking of him, not herself. How typically Paige. "And I meant it. Not because I don't want you. But because I don't *want* to want you."

"I know everything's complicated. I know I might be leaving, by why can't—"

"I don't want to hurt you."

"What makes you think you will?"

"I don't believe you're the type of woman who just wants a fling, a satisfaction of physical needs. And that's all I can offer you." He must have gotten across his point because she didn't protest; she didn't ask any questions.

He wanted to reach for her again but knew he shouldn't. Instead he offered, "But I meant what I said, Paige. If you need to talk, I'll listen."

She squared her shoulders and tried to blank the emotions from her eyes. "I can talk to Doc."

She was choosing to withdraw from him, and he supposed that was best for both of them. He hoped he'd given her the comfort she'd needed for the moment. That was all he could do.

A few minutes later, after Clay had gone, Paige folded her mother's letter and stuffed it into its envelope. Her fingers trembled. Clay's kiss had done something the first kiss hadn't. It had made her realize she could depend on Clay, she could lean on Clay, she could talk to Clay, she could love Clay. She was falling in love with Clayton Reynolds and that idea scared her even more than the passionate feelings he aroused in her. What in heaven's name was she going to do about it?

EIGHT

The next evening, Clay pushed his cart through the grocery store, thinking about Paige—the tears in her eyes, the confusion in her voice, the fact that she might soon leave Langley.

There was no point chewing on it. It seemed Paige's parents had controlled her motivation and dreams from when she was born. Could she battle that and do what was right for herself? What was right might be going back to Africa, would most likely be going back to Africa. Change was difficult. Humans were creatures of habit. Habit for Paige was mirroring her parents' aspirations.

Clay took two boxes of linguini from the shelf next to him and dumped them into his cart. As he pushed the vehicle forward, he spotted Ben coming toward him. He stopped.

Ben seemed embarrassed as he gestured toward his cart. "Mom made me stop and get stuff for supper."

Clay shrugged. "It's something I have to do if I want to eat." He glanced at the cane in Ben's cart. "How's it going?"

"It's going. Mom and Dad are pushing me to apply to colleges for the second semester."

"Are you going to?"

"I can't see the point. I don't know what I want to do. I don't want to feel guilty about Dad going into debt. It all seems pointless."

Ben had to find a focus, some goal that would drive him past his disability. "Don't give up the idea without careful thought. Education will give you an edge others don't have."

Ben's brows drew together. "You go to college?"

Clay nodded.

"What for?"

"Electrical engineering."

Ben's surprise was obvious. "Then what are you doing in Langley when you could be working in some big city?"

"I choose to be here, Ben."

"Because of your accident?"

"Yes."

Ben gave him a speculative look. When another shopper came down the aisle, Ben said, "I gotta go. Maybe I'll see you around."

Clay nodded again.

When Clay went home, he stowed away the groceries, then dialed Doc's number. Paige answered.

"I happened to see Ben and he sounds as if he's giving up the idea of going to college."

"That's what his counselor says, too. She's disappointed because his interest surveys were revealing and strongly suggested a specific direction."

"What was it?"

"The sciences. It seems Ben has excellent background knowledge, especially in biology."

"Damn!"

"I know. It will be a waste if he doesn't go. But maybe in another six months . . ."

Clay wanted to punch something or at least shake some sense into one stubborn teenager. "It'll be even further out of his mind. He's worried about his dad going into debt. What if I set up a scholarship fund to get him started?''

The silence lasted so long, Clay asked, "Paige?''

"Why do you want to do that?''

"Because it would get him going in the right direction.''

"Ben doesn't need the money as much as he needs motivation. Can't you see that?''

"He needs both.''

"Would that be the easy way out for you?''

The truth jabbed Clay's conscience and he couldn't get angry with Paige for seeing it. "I want to help him.''

"Then share your recuperation process with him. Get involved in his life.''

"You don't know what you're asking.''

Her voice was gentle. "Tell me.''

"I can't.''

He heard her sigh. "Money isn't enough, Clay. I suppose you could talk to Ben about it, but don't be surprised if it doesn't make a difference. I think he's just using it as an excuse. With his intelligence and grades, he can probably get a grant or scholarship from one of the private colleges.''

Clay hadn't known they were that readily available. "I see.''

"Do you, Clay? The other night I poured out my fears to you. I trusted you. Can't you trust me?''

He knew she was hurt that he wouldn't confide in her. But if he did confide in her, they could both get hurt even more. "I told you I'll listen whenever you want to talk. But don't expect me to bare my soul just because you did.''

"I never thought you'd be insensitive, Clay, but that statement of yours just proved me wrong.'' And with that, she hung up the phone with a decisive click.

Clay stared at the dead line. He wished he could tell her her kisses set him on fire, made him burn to possess her—not just her body, but all of her. And he wished he could confide in her. But he was afraid that would be an end, not a beginning. He'd handled enough endings for a lifetime; he wasn't about to add one more to the list.

Paige stabbed at the packed earth as if it were the enemy.

Suddenly a shadow blocked the sun from shining over her shoulder. "Are you weeding or working off frustration?"

Paige sat back on her heels and looked up at Doc. "A little of both." She sighed and then admitted, "A lot of both. I just talked to Clay. Sometimes he makes me so angry."

"And other times?"

She couldn't fool Doc. She never could. "And other times I like him so much, I wonder what it would be like to—" She stopped abruptly.

"Love him?"

She took off her gloves and set them on the ground beside her. "Bad timing, isn't it? Clay won't open up to me. Apparently he doesn't feel nearly as much as I do."

Doc shook his head. "That might not be a valid conclusion."

She closed her eyes for a moment. "If he cared about me, he could talk to me."

"The one might not have anything to do with the other."

She opened her eyes and protested, "Well, it *should*."

Doc chuckled at her indignation. "Because *you* think it should?"

Her shoulders slumped. "Oh, Doc. I told him why I came here. About the children. And he was so supportive, comforting. But then other times he's as distant as the farthest star. I just wish I could understand. Can't you tell me what happened to him to make him this way?"

"You know I can't tell you what Clay's told me in confidence. But I can tell you one thing: He's been hurt badly—physically and emotionally. As I said before, I don't think even I know the whole story. But I do know he's faced rejection, lots of it."

"Involving women?"

With his sneaker, Doc shoved a clump of dirt back into the flower bed. "I think that's only part of it. It's no secret he dated a woman in Langley a couple of years ago. It seemed serious. They went everywhere together. But then overnight . . . I don't know what happened."

"She's still in Langley?"

"No. I heard she took a job in Baltimore. She had no family here, so she never came back."

Paige picked up the gloves and gardening fork she'd been using. "Clay was right."

"About what?"

She stood. "Everyone knows everything about everybody."

Doc nodded. "I suppose so. Several people have commented about you and Clay seeing each other."

She took a step back. "We aren't! We haven't even been on a real date."

Doc smiled broadly. "And what's a real date?"

She stooped and grabbed the sheaf of newspaper she'd used to cushion her knees. "You're not so old you can't remember. Dinner, a movie maybe, no one else around."

"You'd like that?"

She met Doc's gaze. "Very much. Maybe too much. Maybe it's not a good idea at all."

"Paige, I'm just going to say one thing, and then you can make up your own mind. Clay's been hurt and it's hard for him to trust. If you want his trust, you might have to give him your heart. Are you ready to do that? Because if you're not, you'd better leave him alone."

On Wednesday, Paige was still mulling over Doc's words as she treated her patients and escorted the last one out to the receptionist's desk early that evening. Tomorrow she and Clay were supposed to shop for supplies for the Fourth of July. Would he remember?

Paige said good-bye to her patient. Her receptionist nodded to the waiting room. Ben sat there, staring out the window. Paige knew he didn't have an appointment. As she walked toward him, he turned and saw her. His smile was uncertain.

"Is something wrong?"

He shrugged. "No. Not exactly. I wondered if you'd take me to Mr. Reynolds's place. I'd like to talk to him."

Paige glanced at her watch. "Now?"

"If you can. I walked into town and went to the store, but they said he'd left early."

"You walked from home?"

"It's only two miles. But my leg's kinda weak now and I knew I'd have trouble getting back. If you can't take me, I'll call my dad to come get me."

"It's not that I can't . . ." She just wasn't sure she wanted to see Clay. She didn't even know if he was at home. Yet this seemed important to Ben, and she sensed he didn't want to see Clay alone. After all, he could've had his father drive him out in the first place.

She took her stethoscope from around her neck. "Give me a few minutes to straighten up my desk and we'll go. Do your parents know where you are?"

He looked sheepish. "No. Mom went shopping and Dad wasn't home yet."

"Call them and tell them I'll bring you home."

Ben grinned and nodded.

Clay nailed the final crossbeam onto the upright post. He'd finally gotten around to mending the fence. At least now he didn't have to worry about Shep running into the barbed wire.

Clay's thumb hurt and he realized he'd caught a splinter. He'd take care of that later. He hated wearing gloves because they interfered too much. He remembered the first time he'd gotten grease all over his hands, how strangely good it had felt. How honest and natural.

He'd finished an afternoon of social studies, science, and a second session of math. His brain had been fuzzy with all the information he was absorbing like a thirsty sponge. The doctors had told him he'd learn quickly. And he had in the two years after the accident. But there were days when the books seemed to take control of his life.

His mother was a wonderful teacher. Patient. Understanding. And too many times to count, he'd wished he could remember the years when she'd nurtured and cared for him in other ways. After he came home from the hospital, he'd given her some bad times with episodes of swearing and mood swings, both common in head-injury patients. Somehow she'd taken it in stride, as had Trish, and helped him work through it.

That particular day, he'd felt claustrophobic in the house, so he'd taken a walk, then wandered into the garage. The riding mower had caught his attention. The weekend before, his dad had cursed at it because it had stalled in the middle of the backyard.

Clay turned the key in the ignition and nothing happened. Seeing the manual for the machine lying on a ladder, he'd paged through it. The mower couldn't be that complicated.

First, he charged the battery. When he tried the ignition again, the mower still wouldn't turn over. Rummaging in a box on a shelf, he found new spark plugs. He changed those. He turned the key in the ignition and it still wouldn't start.

It seemed only logical that he check the wiring next. When he did, he found the problem. Following the wire to the starter under the seat, he realized the weight of the rider was supposed to bring the seat into contact with the switch. It wasn't making that contact because a bolt was missing and the starter had slipped.

Searching in his father's nails and bolts, he found one to fit. With the starter properly attached, the mower started when he turned the key.

That had been the beginning. His mother hadn't simply taught him material he'd forgotten; she'd taught him problem-solving techniques through basic geometry, the scientific method, and simple stick-to-it-iveness. That evening Clay had gone to the library and taken out every book he could find on basic mechanics. Then he'd started overhauling neighbors' mowers. After two years of rehabilitating his mind and body, he'd found a job at a farm center, repairing and reconditioning garden equipment. He'd listened, learned, and finally decided it was time to move on, time to move up, time to take control of his life and make it what he wanted.

And seven years later, what had he accomplished? He had a life of his own, he had friends, he felt he belonged. But did he really, when no one knew the honest-to-God's truth about him?

What would Paige do if he told her? Would she run? Would she back off? Would she think he was a freak like the tabloid reporter who'd somehow managed to get into his home after his accident?

Shep barked from inside the house. Clay had thought it would be safer to fix the fence with the dog inside. But when Shep barked, there was a good reason.

Clay picked up the hammer and nails and strode toward the house. Halfway across the yard, he saw Paige and Ben. His stomach tightened and his heart beat more rapidly.

Paige looked beautiful as always. Her pale blue blouse and navy linen skirt might have looked ordinary on anyone else. On her, the severity added to her sleek lines, her graceful walk.

Ben looked tentative, but Paige hung back to let the

teenager approach first. He stuffed one hand in his pocket and gripped his cane tightly with the other. "Mr. Reynolds, can we talk?"

Clay tried to prepare himself for whatever was coming. "Come into the house."

They walked toward the back door. Ben went inside first. When Clay held the door for Paige, she shook her head. "I'm going for a walk to give you some privacy."

Ben looked worried. "Dr. Conrad, you don't have to go."

She smiled. "Clay knows how to listen, Ben. You didn't come here to talk to me."

Clay said, "Go on into the living room. I'll be there in a minute." When Ben was out of earshot, he asked, "What's up?"

"I'm not sure. He just said he wanted to see you." Paige touched Clay's arm. "Go easy, okay?"

Clay pulled back defensively, as much from the power of her touch as from her comment. "Why did you bring him here if you don't trust me with him?"

She released his arm. "I trust you with him. It's just that I think he's ready to start thinking about the future and he needs guidance, not scolding."

After a brief, taut silence, Clay asked, "And why do you think I can guide him?"

"Because whatever happened to you, whatever you've been through, you survived, you came out strong. Ben needs to know how to do that."

Clay didn't feel strong right now. He felt as if he were perched on the edge of the mountain, ready to tumble over the rim. "You expect too much."

"No, I think you expect too little."

And with that, Paige headed across the yard. She stopped and turned. "If you let Shep out, I'll take him for a walk."

The dog must have been sitting behind the door. At the

sound of his name, he barked. Clay opened the screen
door and Shep came bounding out.

As the dog barreled toward Paige, Clay was afraid he'd
jump up and knock her down. But he merely stopped by
her side. She crouched down, petted and talked to the
animal, then stood.

Clay shook his head. She had a way with people; she
had a way with animals. She had a way with *him*. He
thought he'd take some hits about their phone conversation, but she hadn't mentioned it and he felt guilty as hell.

He rubbed the back of his neck and went inside.

Ben had picked up the wildlife book on the coffee table
and was paging through it. When he saw Clay, he closed
it and replaced it.

Clay didn't know how to put the teenager at ease when
he was feeling so uneasy himself. He sat on the sofa and
stretched his arm across its back. "What did you want to
talk about?"

"Tell me about your accident."

Clay had thought they'd talk about Ben's future, not
Clay's past. He smiled wryly. "You want to trade war
stories?"

"I want to know how bad it was. I want to know what
you went through, how you felt."

Clay pulled in a deep breath. "I don't remember the
accident per se."

"You don't? Man, I remember that car getting too
close. . . ." Ben cringed.

"It's not unusual for head . . . uh, for accident victims
to blank out the trauma of the accident. I remember waking up on the ledge, so filled with pain I couldn't breathe,
I couldn't think. I didn't know where I was. There were
helicopters. Somehow the rescue team got me onto a
stretcher and into the copter. I don't remember much about
the next few days. The doctors kept me drugged because
of the pain." No one had realized until the drugs had
worn off that Clay didn't know his name or the people

around his bed or his birth date. And at first, the doctors had believed once he recovered from the concussion, he'd get back to normal.

Ben's eyes were wide with interest. "So, did you go straight to rehab or home?"

"I started rehabilitation a week after surgery. But I didn't go to a hospital like you did. I went to out-patient physical therapy every day."

"They told me the hospital helps you recover faster."

"That's probably true." But Clay's family had been more concerned about his mental rehabilitation. His mother and Trish had begun working with him as soon as he was home. Thank God they hadn't waited for the recovery the doctors had first predicted.

Ben elbowed the throw pillow in back of him to the corner of his chair. "Did they constantly push you to do more, to do better?"

He remembered not being able to lift his arm to comb his hair. He remembered not being able to read a written page. "I pushed myself, Ben. I wanted a life again even if it didn't include climbing rocks."

"So why didn't you go back to engineering? You said that's what you studied."

Clay shifted on the sofa. He didn't want to lie to Ben, but he wasn't ready to divulge everything. So he told him the truth as he saw it. "Anything serious—accidents, the loss of someone you love, anything that shakes up your life—makes you think differently. I could have died on that ledge. I could have died during surgery or in intensive care. Just facing that made me reexamine everything."

Ben clearly didn't understand. "Like what?"

"What I wanted to do with the rest of my life. I'd been given a second chance, Ben. And I could do anything I wanted within my capabilities. I no longer wanted to spend my life cooped up in an office, only really being free to breathe on weekends. The rock climbing had been an escape to break out of a life my father had molded for me."

He and Trish had figured that out, one of the many times they'd discussed the *old* Clay.

"You didn't want to be an engineer?"

"I had the ability and the intelligence, and my father wanted me as his partner in his business."

Ben frowned. "You were railroaded."

Clay smiled at Ben's perception. "I didn't know it at the time. I was doing what was expected of me. I guess at eighteen I didn't think I had a choice. But you do. You can do anything you want."

Ben looked at his sneakers and rubbed his toe against the fringe of the rug. "Except play football."

"Except play football," Clay agreed, realizing Ben was finally letting go of his dream.

Ben rubbed his palm over the knee of his jeans. "It's so hard, you know? I've never thought of doing anything else. Football's all that mattered."

"But you were going to go to college. What were you going to major in?"

"I wasn't. I didn't have to declare until I was a junior. I don't even know if I want to go to college now. Four more years of school. What's the point?"

Ben was beginning to change his thinking, but not enough to think of the future. "The point is you need a good education so you'll have future options."

"I'm having enough trouble with getting through right now, Mr. Reynolds, let alone five years from now. I could start working somewhere, making money so I can get a car."

"Ben, you have to look ahead."

"I don't want to look ahead. That's all I did with football was look ahead so I could play pro ball some day." He paused for a moment. "Don't you get mad? So damn mad at what you don't have anymore, what you could have had?"

"Yes, I get mad. But not as much as I used to. What

good does it do? Getting angry doesn't change the way things are.''

Ben's shoulders hunched. ''I just want to punch something sometimes, or scream until the whole world hears.''

Clay knew that feeling all too well. In fact every time he thought about Paige, he wished . . . What? That the accident had never happened? That his life could be as normal as the next person's? That he could tell Paige about the amnesia and she wouldn't look at him as if he were some kind of freak?

Ben's voice intruded on the questions. And added one more. ''Mr. Reynolds, is your life as good now as it was before your accident?''

How could Clay answer that when he couldn't remember life before the accident? ''It's different. Not better or worse, but different. You can make your life anything you want it to be.''

Ben pulled his left leg into the sofa and eyed it disdainfully. ''I just wish my leg would work better . . . more.''

''Give it time.''

''Didn't you get tired of waiting to get better?''

''I didn't wait. I did everything I could to make it happen.''

Shep came bounding into the living room from the kitchen and sat in front of Clay, his tail wagging. Clay scratched around the dog's ears.

Paige entered the room and the anger Ben had spoken about, the resentment for circumstances that couldn't be changed, barreled through Clay. He knew he had to do something physical or explode. But he wanted to make sure Ben had asked all his questions.

''Is there anything else, Ben?''

The teenager stood. ''No. I just wondered . . . would it be all right if I talked to you once in a while? It's hard for someone who hasn't gone through this to understand.''

Clay was beginning to feel more and more boxed in.

But he couldn't say no. He knew how important under-standing could be. It meant the difference between accep-tance and rejection.

"I'm usually here in the evenings. Call me at the store or here."

Paige watched the two of them, and Clay suspected she was sizing up their moods. He wanted to ask her to come back after she took Ben home. He wanted to apologize for his harshness the other night, take her in his arms, and kiss her until nothing mattered but the passion between them. But Paige deserved more than passion. She deserved a man who could share her dreams. Clay imagined her married to a doctor, following the road her parents had forged. Jealousy, hot and thick, rippled through him. Yet he couldn't envision her staying in Langley anymore than he could envision her accepting his lack of a past. If his own father couldn't . . .

Paige asked Ben, "Ready?"

"Yeah." He followed her to the door, but he said to Clay, "Thanks."

Clay nodded.

Paige's gaze locked to Clay's and once more he wished he could stop wanting her.

Paige drove Ben home. On her way back to Doc's, she couldn't forget the anguished look in Clay's eyes as she and Ben had left. His words pushed her away, but there was something basic going on between them that had noth-ing to do with the words. Paige almost felt he was reach-ing out to her, yet when she reached back, he withdrew. Why? Before she thought better of it, she made a U-turn and let her heart lead her back to the man who held the answer to her question.

Ben had told her about his conversation with Clay, and in her opinion, the visit had helped the teenager simply because he felt someone understood. At this moment, she was more concerned about Clay. It was obvious he didn't believe anyone could understand. Understand what, she didn't know. But the story Clay had related to Ben was the edited version. She was sure of it.

Clay was holding a secret, something that was eating him up. And she cared about him too much to let him do that to himself.

She knocked on the front door. Shep barked, but Clay didn't come. When she turned the knob, the door opened and she stepped inside. Shep rubbed his head against her knee.

"Where is he, boy?"

Shep whined and pattered into the kitchen. She followed. The back door stood open and she could hear a thudding sound.

When she looked through the screen door, she could see Clay at the back corner of the lot by the woodpile, his shirt off, an ax in his hands. His shirt lay on the ground by the fence as if it had been tossed there quickly. Even from a distance, he looked upset.

She didn't know what she was going to say to him; she just had to go to him.

As she walked toward him, her breath caught in her chest. His bronze skin glistened in the last rays of light. He stood against the descending sun, his profile strong and determined and true. When he raised his arms, his muscles rippled. He brought down the ax with a sharp, powerful stroke. Then he brought it down again and again. The log split and fell. He let it lay, stooped, hefted another log onto the splitting block, and with the same, sure rhythm, raised the ax and lowered it again.

Clay was oblivious to his surroundings. His face was etched with concentration, telling her he was more than upset. He looked angry enough to fell a tree with his bare hands. His expression was taut, strained, filled with pain.

He didn't hear her approach as he split another log, then another. Closer now, Paige waited. When he lowered the ax and paused for a second, she moved. He saw her the same moment her fingers went around his forearm. The damp heat emanating from him was hot enough to burn her alive. The look on his face should have made her run for cover. But she didn't. She couldn't.

She loved him.

The sweat on Clay's skin trickled into black curling hair. At the lake, she'd wanted to touch it, to touch him.

As she did so now, he pulled back, his voice gravelly. "Go away, Paige."

"No."

Green fire blazed in his eyes, and his gaze settled on her mouth with a fierceness that stole the air from her lungs.

His jaw was tense, the nerve on the right pulsing as she watched him closely. "You're asking for trouble," he bit out.

"No, I'm asking you to let me in."

He swore viciously, dropped the ax, and took her by the shoulders. "You don't know what you're asking."

She didn't waver. "Maybe not. I only know I want to get closer to you."

His mouth came down hard on hers. She could feel his anger, she could feel his frustration, and under it all she knew he would never hurt her. He was fighting, and it was the fighting that made the kiss harsh. He didn't give her time to breathe, pushing his tongue between her lips. She didn't pull away; she didn't fight back.

Her acquiescence seemed to make him angrier. His hands left her shoulders and he held her face, angling it so he could take more, go deeper. She felt him shudder when her tongue stroked his. The tension in his body surrounded her but didn't invade her.

Roughly, he tore his mouth from hers. "Damn it, Paige. You shouldn't be here." His voice was coarse and filled with pain, his breathing ragged.

She reached up and stroked his face. "But I *am* here because that's exactly where I want to be."

With a low groan, he took her mouth again. The fierce passion was still there. The anger wasn't. She wrapped her arms around his back and held on tight.

NINE

Clay's second kiss was pure fire. Streams of it zipped through Paige, weakening her arms and legs. She sought to get her strength back by touching him, by filling her hands with the heat of his back, the texture of his slick skin. She stroked, and he dragged her closer. His large hands caressed her back, found her bottom, and cupped her.

She felt his hard need through his jeans, through her skirt. It scared her but excited her, too. She'd never wanted a man this way; she'd never needed a man this way. Her inexperience didn't seem to matter because her body knew exactly what her emotions had already realized. She wanted to be one with this man. She wanted to fall into his soul, surround herself with him, and find fulfillment. It had nothing to do with experience, everything to do with feeling and being.

Need licked inside her as her tongue dueled with his and she arched into him.

Frantically, he pulled at her blouse. The silky material slid above her skirt. He unfastened her bra. Not taking his mouth from hers, he tried to undo the buttons. First one, then another, until she felt his hands on her stomach. He caressed with his thumbs, his rough skin making each stroke more sensual. He became impatient when he couldn't touch enough. Buttons popped. His hand closed over her full breast. He circled it with his open hand, then closed over it again.

She pressed into his hand, needing more.

He understood her need. He slid his open fingers back and forth over her nipple, creating an exquisite friction that created fiery desire within her. All strength seemed to seep out of her. She clung to Clay, immobilized by his seductive caress. Until he took her nipple between his thumb and forefinger.

Too many erotic sensations barraged Paige, sensations that were primitive, awe-inspiring, frightening in their newness. She pressed into Clay and rocked her hips against his.

He groaned, broke their kiss, and pulled her down to the ground. His eyes were wild with hunger, desperate with need. She knew because she felt it, too.

His kisses were hot, open-mouthed, as he tasted her neck, throat, the valley between her breasts. The grass was soft under her, the sun's heat still warming it. Dusk, earth, the scents of passion went to her head, making her world spin.

He touched her nipple with his thumb again and she cried out. The sensation was so consuming, so erotic, so unlike anything she'd ever felt, she didn't know whether to embrace it or escape it. But when his lips instead of his finger touched the nipple, her hands closed around blades of grass and squeezed from the sheer sensation of spiraling pleasure.

His tongue was rough, soft, teasing, merciless. Her broken gasp was almost a sob. Never had she known anything like this.

Clay lifted his head, saw the need on her face, then lowered his mouth to her other breast. Paige laced her fingers in his hair and held him to her. His lips surrounded her, his tongue rasped over her, his scorching breath taunted her.

She grabbed his shoulders, aware of the power in his muscles, his strength, his maleness. He shuddered as her fingers kneaded. He came to her mouth again and sheathed her body under his, then pressed his knee between her legs. The stimulation was almost more than she could assimilate as he probed her mouth, palmed her breast, and pressed where she wanted to feel pressure most.

She might be a virgin, but she was also a doctor, and she understood what her body craved. Nothing seemed more important. Not the future, not Clay's secret, not her confusion about the direction of her life. She and Clay were here, now, that was all that mattered.

She clutched at him. She wanted more and didn't know how to get it. His chest was steamy hot, silky slick, and roughly textured by hair. She rubbed her shoulder against him since she couldn't move much else. At the same time, she roamed her hands down his sides until she met the waistband of his jeans. She slid along it until she reached the snap in front.

He still drugged her with kisses, long and deep, until she was dizzy. Feeling her hand at his waist, he shifted until she cupped him in her palm through his jeans. He shuddered again as she held him, then stroked up and down as best she could between them.

Clay was gone, so far gone. From the first touch of her fingers on his arm, her refusal to leave, the hungry need in her eyes. Her lips were sweet, the inside of her mouth food and drink for a hungry and thirsty man. He wanted to devour her, assuage the need she'd incited from the first time he'd seen her. He'd given her the chance to leave; he'd given her the chance to run. But she'd chosen to stay. And that, even more than his ferocious desire for her, had broken his control.

The first touch of her tongue had made him more aroused than he ever imagined he could be. And when he'd taken the rosy velvet tip of her breast into his mouth, he thought he'd die from the throbbing ache of needing her. Her keening moans inflamed him further until he wanted his hands all over her, his tongue deep in her mouth, his hunger appeased any way he could accomplish it.

She had eased the hunger but also made it worse. Her fingers in his hair, her hands on his back, her skin against his chest created desire like he'd never known it. He was on fire and didn't know if he wanted to put it out.

Paige twisted beneath him and he realized she was trying to undo his fly. The thought of her soft, warm hands on him made him break off the kiss and raggedly gulp in air.

She murmured a protest and moved restlessly. Then she turned her head, searching for his mouth. When she couldn't find it, she opened her eyes. "I want you, Clay. Please make love to me."

Want. Love. Paige. Reality splashed him, as cold as the lake water in December. What in God's name was he doing? The blue of her eyes, the softness of her hands, the tremendous caring within her had stripped his defenses until he'd forgotten restraint and let frustration and need take over. They were on the grass in his backyard, for Christ's sake. What had happened to him?

He rolled away from her and pushed himself up to an upright position, not trusting himself to look at her naked breasts or gaze into her dazed blue eyes. His urgent arousal abated somewhat as he took deep, full breaths to maintain some type of control.

She reached for him. "Clay, what's wrong?"

When her fingers closed around his arm, he snapped, "Don't touch me, Paige. Don't make me regret this more than I do."

She didn't let go. "I want you, Clay."

His eyes met hers then, and he couldn't deal with the

depth of feeling he found there. He lifted her hand from his arm and held her by the wrist. "You don't know me."

She searched his face, then pulled her hand from his grasp. All the emotion he'd seen in her eyes coalesced into anger as she levered herself up. "And whose fault is that?"

When he didn't respond, she made a soft noise of frustration. Fastening her bra, she pulled her blouse around her and realized buttons were missing. Her already flushed cheeks turned redder. With an attempt at modesty, she took the ends of the blouse and tied them together at her waist. The result was deep cleavage but adequate coverage.

She scrambled to her feet and attempted to swipe the grass from her skirt. Giving up, she started across the yard and left Clay sitting there. She didn't look back.

Paige opened her eyes the next morning and groaned. She might have gotten about two hours' sleep. Damn Clay Reynolds. Damn the daylights out of him. He was stubborn, frustrating, sexy, strong . . . and she loved him. Tears pricked her eyes. How stupid for this to happen now.

When would be any better, though, since she was constantly picking up and moving on? What kind of personal life could she have? Her work meant everything to her, didn't it?

Maybe Clay was right to push her away. If she gave him her heart, what would happen if she left?

The phone rang and her heart lurched. Ten to one she knew who it was. She lifted the receiver on her nightstand.

Clay's voice was low and morning-husky. "Paige?"

She came to a sitting position and put the phone on her lap. "Yes?"

"If you have more important things to do today, I can go to Westminster and get what we need for the Fourth."

She knew he expected her to jump at the chance not to be with him, to escape the awkwardness last night had caused. Well, she wouldn't give him that satisfaction. Awkwardness wouldn't kill her. "Actually, I saved other shopping for today, too. I haven't been to the mall in a couple of weeks."

"I see."

She doubted it. She decided to offer him an escape route if he wanted it. "I suppose I could get what we need, but you know more about it. Unless you want to give me the sizes, the amounts—"

"No. I'm not going to heap that on your shoulders. What time should I pick you up?" He sounded as if it was the last thing on earth he wanted to do.

"I should finish at the hospital about two. Is two-thirty all right?"

"It's fine. I'll see you then."

When Paige hung up, she knew it wasn't fine. Clay didn't want to see her. He didn't want to be near her. Somehow she'd just have to live with that.

You can't die from awkwardness, Paige told herself for at least the hundredth time. But she didn't know if she believed it. Except for a perfunctory greeting, Clay had been silent during the drive. Then, of course, so had she. This situation was beyond her social expertise.

Sitting next to Clay in silence, watching his long fingers on the wheel, aware of the tilt of his elbow, the tautness of his thigh as he moved his foot from the gas to the brake, made breathing difficult. She couldn't stop thinking about his lips on hers, his hand on her breast, the shivers of excitement she'd felt in his arms.

Obviously, Clay had already managed to forget. But she couldn't. Not in this lifetime. Maybe what had happened was old hat to him, but it wasn't to her. Irritation bubbled inside her. How could he pretend it never happened?

Clay parked the Blazer. Paige hopped out quickly so he wouldn't think she was waiting for him to open the door for her. He held the door for her at the entrance. Inadvertently, her arm brushed his ribs as she passed him. A shock forked through her. Her eyes never met his. She got as far as his jaw, saw the tense set and the nerve jumping, looked straight ahead, and walked into the tiled thoroughfare.

Paige let Clay lead. He wore jeans and a red-and-white-striped polo shirt, looking crisp and sharp, not as if he'd come straight from work. She pictured him without the shirt, all bronze skin and hard physique. Then stopped the pictures.

The T-shirt shop was empty except for the proprietor. Clay explained what they had in mind. The man showed them two styles—V neck and crew neck.

Paige looked up at Clay. "Which do you think would be better?"

"Whichever you pick is fine."

She chose the V neck.

The proprietor asked which style of printing they preferred. When Paige asked Clay's opinion, again he said, "Whichever you think will work best."

Paige's temper had a long fuse, but it was shortened a great deal by Clay's rejection last night, by his silence on the ride to Westminster, and now by his let's-hurry-up-and-get-this-over-with attitude. She chose the block printing.

Then they had to choose the colors. When Clay shrugged, Paige said sarcastically, "Fuchsia on yellow would be nice."

Clay scowled.

"Would you prefer something else?" she asked sweetly.

Hot desire leapt in his eyes and his gaze scorched her.

She cleared her throat and said to the man behind the counter, "Better make it red on white." Her fingers trembled. She curled them into her palms and took her hands from the countertop.

After the proprietor took the appropriate information for the order, Clay said briskly, "Balloons next. There's a party store about halfway down the mall."

They walked in silence, entered the store, and found the balloons easily. Paige reached for a bag of assorted colors at the same time as Clay. Their fingers brushed.

Paige swallowed hard. Clay pulled back his hand.

"Clay . . ."

"What?" His tone was sharp and clipped.

"Why did you come today if you didn't want to?"

"It wasn't a matter of wanting."

She didn't miss the double meaning. "Well, maybe it should be."

After a taut silence, he said, "I wasn't going to leave you with the responsibility of taking care of this."

She pointed out, "I'm competent enough to order T-shirts, especially when you don't give a hoot what I order."

His eyes became a dangerous green. "Don't push me, Paige."

A temper she didn't know existed exploded. "Don't push you, don't touch you. Why don't you simply close yourself up in your house and not let anybody in? It would keep you safe."

He looked as shocked at her explosion as she was that she'd let it loose. Slowly, in an even tone he asked, "What do you want from me?"

She wasn't sure. Since she'd realized she loved him, she wanted the freedom to explore the feelings. But Clay would never accept that. "A little honesty would be nice."

"You want honesty?" He cupped her chin firmly in his hand. "I want you so damn bad I can't see straight. I hear your voice, I see your hair slide along your cheek, I feel your fingers on my arm and all I think about is taking you to bed."

His gruff, low voice brushed over each and every one of

her disconcerted nerve endings, awakening and thrilling, scaring and exciting. Heat rushed to her cheeks then settled in a much more private place.

Keeping her hypnotized by his green gaze, he asked, "Is that honest enough for you?"

She didn't have an answer. She couldn't think.

With a frustrated sigh, he released her, ran his hand through his hair and snatched up two bags of balloons.

Clay paid for the balloons and they left the store. At the threshold to the mall, he stopped.

Paige took his arm, well aware of what he'd said about her touching him. She felt his muscles tense. "Why are you so angry?"

His gaze locked to hers. "I'm not angry with you."

"It seems as if you are."

"Before you came to town, my life was perfectly acceptable. Comfortable. Uneventful."

"And now?"

"It couldn't get more uncomfortable."

She didn't understand what was causing so much turmoil for him, but it certainly sounded as if he was sorry he'd ever met her. That hurt. She turned away from him. "I'm sorry."

He must have heard the quiver in her voice. He clasped her shoulder. "Paige, look at me."

She did.

"Are you going back to Africa?"

"I don't know." She studied Clay's face, the tiny lines, the heavy brows, the sensual mouth. "Why can't we enjoy what we have now?" She couldn't believe she was being this bold, but she wanted to hang on to the specialness between her and Clay. She didn't want him to toss it aside because it wasn't convenient. The one thing she'd learned in Africa above all else was that each day was precious and she couldn't take any of them for granted.

Clay traced her cheekbone. "Ah, Paige. You make me

want. You make me need. I look at you, spend time with you, and I almost want to take a chance.''

She covered his hand with hers, loving his touch, loving the feel of him. ''Why can't you?''

''I don't want either of us to get hurt. Have you ever been hurt by someone you cared about?''

She felt sheltered, naive, much too innocent at this moment. If she could say, ''Yes, and I overcame the experience,'' she'd have ammunition. All she had were her growing feelings for Clay, so she dropped her hand and answered, ''No.''

He took his hand from her cheek and hooked his thumb in his belt loop. ''It's no picnic, Paige. When you care too much, and something happens . . . hearts don't mend without leaving nasty scars.''

''Believe me, Clay, I know there are no guarantees. On anything. We're given one moment at a time.''

The elongated lines around his eyes manifested the strain inside him. ''I don't know if that's enough. I don't know if a few weeks are worth the pain.''

''Maybe the joy's worth it.''

''And maybe you're a dreamer. There are so many variables, so many things that can go wrong.''

''And so many things that can go right.''

He almost smiled then. Almost. He looked as if he might lean forward and kiss her. But he didn't. He shifted away from her. ''What else do you need to buy?''

His change of subject threw her off balance. ''What?''

He did smile then and her heart skipped. ''You said you hadn't been to the mall for a couple of weeks. What else do you need?''

At least some of the tension between them had eased. She wasn't sure why, but she was glad. She'd rather they talk; she'd rather he confide in her. But being with him was enough for now. ''Writing paper. And I want to buy Doc some new towels for the bathroom. He hasn't replaced his in years. I need perfume, too.'' She had never worn perfume abroad. She loved wearing it now.

"Then let's go to the department store."

"Clay, I know men don't like to shop. If you want to meet me somewhere in a little while . . .''

"Who said men don't like to shop?"

She smiled. "I thought it was common knowledge."

"Another misconception someone spread about men. It isn't that we don't like to shop. We like to shop for different things than women. You should see the men who come into my store, examine every piece of machinery twice, buy something, and still come back in a week to look at everything again." Clay's eyes twinkled. "We just prefer not to shop in the lingerie department. It does something to our image."

"So as long as I don't drag you through nightgowns, you have no problem?"

"It's definitely not a good idea to drag me through nightgowns."

The knowing in his eyes almost undid her because they were both imagining the same thing. She took a deep breath. "Let's go."

Clay had slowed his stride and as they passed an ice cream concession, he caught her elbow. "How about an ice cream cone? It's been a long time since lunch."

She smiled. "Sounds good."

They bought the cones and sat in the middle of the mall to enjoy them. Clay asked her, "Have you heard from Ben?"

She shook her head. "Have you?"

Clay should never have suggested ice cream. But then the most simple things with Paige took on an entirely different meaning. Clay couldn't take his eyes from her as her tongue twirled and caught a drop of ice cream on the side of her cone. She licked the side of her mouth.

His gut clenched. "Uh, no."

Clay was fascinated by the way Paige's right brow

raised as she bit into her cone, the way her tongue twirled into the small spaces in the bottom. Her silky hair swayed against her cheek as she tilted her head. Her stunning blue eyes were soft and liquid and she'd never looked more lovely, even with the smudge of chocolate on her nose.

Feeling Clay's gaze on her, Paige looked at him. He rubbed his thumb gently across the tip of her nose, then licked the ice cream from his finger.

She didn't look away and he had to touch her again. For too long he'd kept his distance. For too long he'd denied his need. He trailed his finger down the side of her cheek and he felt her shiver. Lord, why couldn't he just take her to bed, live for now? She was willing.

Why couldn't he? Because it wasn't honest. He couldn't make love to her without telling her the truth. She wasn't the kind of woman you made love to and kept your distance from.

Clay removed his hand from her cheek. She was looking at him expectantly and he wanted to pull her into his arms, but . . .

Her beeper went off. Paige switched it off and murmured, "I have to get to a phone."

She didn't hesitate; she didn't think about herself first and what was being interrupted. Her patients came first. Her healing came first. And he'd hoped she wouldn't go back to Africa? *Dream on, Reynolds.*

He showed her where the pay phones were located. She dialed Doc's service.

After a few brief comments, she said, "Tell her to stay calm and I'll be there as soon as I can." Paige turned to Clay. "It's Miriam. She's having sporadic contractions. Nothing less than a half hour apart, though."

"It's too soon, isn't it?"

"She has three weeks until her delivery date, but babies don't always read a calendar. I'd like to get to her as soon as I can and check her out."

"I'll drive you. No use taking time to stop at Doc's."

"Thanks, Clay. I owe you one."

He said gruffly, "You don't owe me anything."

When they arrived at Miriam's the woman was obviously upset. "Dr. Conrad, I didn't know what to do. They started about four A.M. I didn't want to call you. . . ."

"I'm glad you did. Let's go to the bedroom and I'll examine you. You remember Clay, don't you?"

"Sure. From your office. Doctor, did I interrupt something? I wouldn't have called, but . . ."

Paige hazarded a quick look at Clay. "You didn't interrupt anything. Let's go to your room and we'll see what this baby's excited about."

Clay watched the two women go to the rear of the first-floor apartment, Paige carrying her black bag. She'd brought it along with her, as always. She always seemed to be prepared.

He looked around curiously. Miriam's sofa was threadbare at the front of the cushions, and Clay suspected she'd purchased it secondhand. The room was immaculate; he didn't see a speck of dust anywhere. Homey touches like embroidered throw pillows, a framed needlepoint, and a colorful afghan thrown over the back of the sofa made the room welcoming. One thing he and Miriam had in common. He didn't see any pictures sitting around. He imagined she didn't want reminders of the husband who'd deserted her. But what about her family?

Clay didn't keep pictures around because he wanted to experience real people, not images. During his rehabilitation, he'd spent hours with family albums, straining to remember. The pictures were just printed images. They meant nothing. He'd memorized faces. Instead of having a picture of Trish or his mother around, he called them, he went to see them. He remembered everything about them in his head. He didn't need a fake reminder.

Clay sat down on a platform rocker.

As often as not recently, his thoughts turned to Paige. She said she owed him. Nothing was further from the truth. Yes, she'd turned his life upside down. But he had to admit he hadn't felt this alive any time he could remember. He grimaced. Alive in very physical ways. But alive emotionally, too. Since Clare, he'd stayed away from women except on the most surface basis. He couldn't seem to stay away from Paige.

Was he headed for disaster? Was he even contemplating telling her about his amnesia? A wave of panic washed over him. Yes, he was.

Like nights when the dreams had plagued him, like the hours when he'd battled his inability to read or the immobility of his shoulder and panic had been a beast ready to devour him, he worked through it. He didn't fight it or try to wish it away. He kept his breathing even and the feeling faded.

He tried to tell himself it didn't matter if Paige couldn't accept his amnesia, if she saw him differently, as less of a man. But it did matter. Way too much for his peace of mind.

She was getting to him in a big way. She'd said she wanted to get closer to him. He wanted to get closer to her. But they were at a standstill until he made some decisions. He couldn't make an impulsive choice. He had to think about more than Paige. If the word got out about his amnesia, his life could be irrevocably changed. Langley might not be such a friendly place. He had a lot to lose, including his financial investment in the store if he decided to move again, if the people of Langley couldn't accept him any better than his neighbors and friends, his father . . . Clare.

No, it wasn't a decision to be made lightly.

When Miriam and Paige emerged from the bedroom, both were smiling.

Clay rose. "Everything all right?"

Paige patted Miriam's shoulder. "False labor pains. But, Miriam, I want you to take it easy. Limit the hours you spend at the sewing machine."

"But I have orders for dresses for a wedding. I have to finish them by next week. And then there are draperies to finish for Mrs. Weaver."

Paige looked worried. "I understand. But if you must work, take planned breaks. Set an alarm. Get up every half hour and get a drink or walk outside. I mean it, Miriam, you have to do this for yourself and your baby."

Clay canvassed the room again. "Miriam, I was noticing your pillows and hangings. Did you do them?"

"Yes. All of them."

"Do you have any more?" Clay asked.

She smiled uncertainly. "A closetful. Why?"

"I know a man in Westminster who has a shop. He sells furniture, but he has a few other crafts, too. I could ask him if he'll put some of your work in the store."

Miriam beamed. "That would be wonderful. I need so many things for the baby. And once it's born, I'm afraid I won't have enough time to work."

"I'll call him this evening and get back to you. In the meantime, you do what Dr. Conrad says. You rest."

"I will." She turned to Paige. "Dr. Conrad, thanks for coming. I'm sorry I messed up your afternoon."

"You didn't mess up anything. If you have any more problems or questions, you call me. Understand?"

Miriam nodded.

As Clay and Paige walked to the Blazer, Paige said, "You did something for Miriam that I couldn't. You relieved some of her worries."

"*If* I can arrange it."

"You will."

TEN

By Friday evening, Clay was restless. Humidity hung in the air outside, not letting the summer temperature drop much even with the onset of evening. Conditions cried out for rain. A storm was brewing, the wind picking up, so he couldn't work outdoors, his basic remedy for pushing away unsettling thoughts.

After their visit to Miriam, Clay had dropped Paige off at Doc's. She'd touched his hand, said, "See you soon," and was gone. He longed to see her soon, he longed to do more than see her, but doubts still ran rampant in his head.

Since then, nothing had held Clay's attention for very long. He'd picked up Miriam's handwork earlier that day and taken it to the shopkeeper in Westminster. Now, stuck in the house, he couldn't decide what to do next. He wandered around the living room, picked up a magazine, and tossed it back to the coffee table. He could go into the store, but that wouldn't keep him from thinking about Paige. His connection to her was Ben. How was the boy doing? What decision had he made about college?

Clay went to the phone. When Ben's mother answered

and learned it was Clay, she said, "I'll get him. Maybe you can talk some sense into him."

What had happened now?

Ben came to the phone. "Hello, Mr. Reynolds."

"Hi, Ben. I wondered how everything was going."

"It's all right."

"Have you made up your mind about college?"

"Yeah. I'm not going."

The teenager's decision surprised Clay. "Ben, if it's the money, don't let that stop you. I could set up a scholarship fund to get you started." He was met by silence. "You wouldn't have to pay it back."

"That's great of you, Mr. Reynolds, but I've made my decision."

Clay heard the intractibility. Where was it coming from? "Why?"

Ben's tone was angry. "Because I'm tired of pushing and pushing. Look how long I've been working on this leg. Months and months. And it's not better."

Clay gentled his tone so he could reason with Ben. "It's better now than when you started, isn't it?"

"But not good enough. Why work for the future when it's never enough?"

"Ben, give it time."

"I'm tired of giving it time. Gus offered me a job at the gas station. In a month, I'll have my diploma. I can work full-time till I save enough for a car, then I can go to Westminster and look for something better."

The naiveté and inexperience of youth, Clay thought. "Like what?"

"Oh, I don't know. Maybe a salesman at a sporting-goods store."

Clay closed his eyes and sighed. "That can't be all you want. Ben, an education can open so many doors. Don't you see that?"

"I see that everyone wants me to do what *they* want me to do. What about what *I* want?"

"What *do* you want?" Clay asked, understanding that was the essence of the problem. Ben didn't know.

"I want my life back. I want everything I lost. But since I can't have that, I'll take what I can get. Right now, a job and some money will do it."

Clay couldn't keep the words from pouring out. "You're being foolish. You don't know what you're throwing away."

"*You* threw away your college education."

"That's entirely different."

"Why?"

"You don't understand, Ben. I had to start over from scratch. You don't. You can go on from here."

"It's my life, Mr. Reynolds, and I'm going to do what I damn well please. I wish everybody would leave me alone."

Clay heard the click of the receiver, the finality of Ben's decision. But Clay couldn't accept the boy's decision. Ben wanted immediate gratification. Life wasn't like that. There was only one way Clay could make the stubborn teenager understand. And if he was going to tell Ben, he might as well tell Paige at the same time. Maybe he was just safeguarding himself against her reaction. He didn't know; he didn't care. He just knew he had to tell Ben how lucky he was and why.

Thunder grumbled as Clay drove to Doc's. There were storm-watch warnings out again. But Clay ignored the cloud-filled, almost-night sky. Even as rain drizzled on the windshield, he didn't give it a second thought. Just as he didn't give a second thought to whether Paige might be out.

He rapped on the door . . . hard. A few moments later she opened it. "Clay." The brightness in her voice vanished when she saw his expression. "What's wrong?"

"Ben's decided he's not going to college. I want you to go with me and convince him otherwise."

"But if his mind's made up—"

"I have a few things to tell him that might change his mind. You need to hear them, too."

She studied Clay for a long moment. "All right. Let me make sure everything's turned off in the kitchen."

The determined purpose on Clay's face almost scared Paige. His defensive stance warned her. What was he going to tell Ben? As Paige climbed in the Blazer, she saw the carton on the backseat and wondered what was in it. She caught a glimpse of shiny gold but couldn't tell what it was.

When Clay took the box from the Blazer, she saw that it held trophies. She glanced at Clay speculatively but didn't ask any questions. He didn't explain.

Ben's mother looked relieved to see them when she answered the door. She waved them to the living room. "Maybe you can change his mind. He won't listen to us. He won't even send in the applications."

"Did something happen?" Paige asked.

"His last few physical therapy sessions haven't gone well and I think he's given up. His father and I don't know what to do for him." She gestured toward the sofa. "Make yourselves comfortable. He's in his room. I'll get him."

Clay set the box on the coffee table. Then Paige watched him pace the room like a caged lion. Thunder boomed outside and the trees shook with sudden gusts of wind as night fell early. The weather seemed to match the turbulence inside Clay. He looked like a thundercloud ready to burst.

Paige crossed to a large aquarium along the side wall of the room. Hoping to distract Clay, she said, "Come look at this."

Clay listened for footsteps on the stairs. Not hearing any, he did as she bid him.

"Look at the anemones. Aren't they beautiful?" The pink and white sea creatures waved their tentacles with the flow of the water. Set against dark rocks, they looked otherworldly. There were a few fish, orange and bright blue, but other sea creatures fascinated Paige more. She pointed to one in between two rocks. "That looks like a feather duster. And there's a blue starfish. This must be a saltwater aquarium. I wonder if Ben set it up. This could be why he did so well on the survey in science, if this type of thing interests him."

Clay ran his hand distractedly through his hair, and Paige knew the last thing he was thinking about was aquariums. How she wished she could read his mind.

Thunder cracked again outside and she jumped. The storm was adding tension to an already tense situation. What was Clay going to reveal? Some of the past she knew nothing about? What could be making him so agitated?

Finally, they heard footsteps. But only Ben came into the living room. He didn't look pleased to see them.

Paige tried for the lighter touch. "I hope we didn't interrupt anything important."

"Nope. I was just reading." Ben glanced uneasily at Clay. "I wish you hadn't come. Nothing you can say will make me change my mind."

Clay's anger was palpable as he went to the coffee table and picked up the carton. Then he crossed to Ben and dumped the contents at the boy's feet. "Look at these, Ben. Each and every one."

Ben didn't dare refuse. He hunched down and examined one after the other. His eyes grew wide. "They all have your name on them. For track. Most of them are for first place." Ben gazed up at Clay. "You won all these?"

"That's what my family tells me."

Ben balanced one in the palm of his hand. "They *tell* you? I don't get it."

Neither did Paige. But she stood by silently, watching and waiting. Her hands shook because she had the foreboding that whatever Clay was going to reveal was no small confidence.

Clay picked up another trophy. "October 1974." He picked up another. "April 1975." And another. "May 1973." He put them back on the pile. "My father says I trained every day, that I worked hard, that I wanted to win as much as he wanted me to win. But I don't remember."

Ben's face was incredulous. "You can't remember winning these? What were you, spaced out on steroids or something?"

Paige sucked in a breath. Is that what Clay couldn't tell her? That he'd been hooked on drugs? But she was a doctor. She could understand—

Clay shook his head. "No drugs, Ben. I don't remember the trophies, I don't remember the races, I don't remember my sixteenth birthday, or my fifteenth, or any before that. I don't remember kissing a girl for the first time, learning to ride a two-wheeler, my mother taking me trick-or-treating, or my sister's dance recital when she was ten. I don't remember anything before my accident and I never will."

After a stunned silence, Ben's exclamation came out as a slow whistle.

In shock, Paige could only stare at Clay and try to understand what he had gone through, what he was still going through.

Clay's feet were spread apart, as if he was bracing himself for their reaction.

Ben sank down into a Queen Anne chair. "You didn't remember your mom or dad?"

Clay stood perfectly still, his arms straight and rigid at his sides. "Or my sister, or my name, or my favorite foods. Not the house I grew up in or the condo I rented."

"Jeez!"

"Ben, I'm not telling you this to impress you. I want you to know how bad an accident can be. Besides not remembering everyday things, I couldn't read or write or do math. I had to learn everything all over."

"You didn't remember anything you learned in high school or college?"

Lightning flashed outside the picture window and the lights flickered. Clay restlessly shifted on his sneakers. "No. That's why I didn't go back to engineering. I spent three years relearning everything. But the hardest part was that I changed. I was not the Clay Reynolds everyone knew. The outward appearance was the same, but not the person inside. Many people couldn't accept that, Ben. I didn't care about rock climbing anymore, I didn't want to sit in an office ten hours a day, monetary success wasn't a goal. Each and every day became a discovery of something I didn't remember, something new and wonderful. But not many people could share that joy."

The magnitude of what Clay was saying hit Paige and her knees wobbled. She sank down on the edge of the sofa.

Clay glanced at her quickly, frowned, then turned back to Ben. "You don't have to start over, Ben. You can make up time and go on. You've spent six months at physical therapy and you think you should be good as new. I spent three years rehabilitating my shoulder and my mind and I still couldn't regain what I lost. I still wake up some mornings, look around, and try to imagine or pray to God that someday I'll have a glimpse of what life used to be. That I'll remember my mother holding me, or Trish fighting with me, or my dad telling me he was proud of me."

Paige was aware of the catch in Clay's voice. She studied his profile, the protective set of his jaw, the serious lines on his brow, and she wanted to hug him more than she wanted to breathe. But he wouldn't accept that here.

He usually spoke only of his sister, not his father or mother. What had his accident done to the family? Is this why he made short visits home? Wanted no pictures sitting around? Paige always heard the strain in Clay's voice as he spoke of his father. What was their relationship now?

Ben asked Clay, "What about your friends? Did they stick by you?"

"No. At first they expected me to remember. Just like my father, they *waited* for me to remember. But they got tired of waiting. We didn't have anything in common. I had a girlfriend at the time of the accident. But at the end of six months, she wanted out. I couldn't remember her or what I used to feel. We were strangers getting to know each other again. She'd liked the idea of a future with an electrical engineer. But at that point, I still couldn't concentrate enough to read an entire magazine, let alone decipher the technical vocabulary of engineering."

"Women are fickle," Ben muttered.

"Women are no different from men. My male friends didn't stick around, either."

Ben lifted his head. "So you do understand."

"I more than understand. I had to move away from my family because everybody looked at me like I was a freak. Even tabloid reporters got wind of it. They heard the word 'amnesia' and they came running."

"Were you in the tabloids?"

"Ben!" Paige protested. She knew what this recital must be costing Clay, and for Ben to ask curious questions seemed almost cruel.

Clay's gaze found hers and seemed to search her. He brushed her protest away with his hand. "It's all right. Yes, I was in the tabloids. At least some made-up story was, that the reporter got from one of my neighbors who didn't know the facts."

"Your picture, too?"

"Yes. Somehow the reporter managed to get it. At that point everything was still so new, so confusing. The photo was lousy but good enough for most of the people in the town to recognize me. You talk about fingers pointing, Ben. I couldn't go to the grocery store, the movies, without people whispering behind their hands and giving me stares like I was from another planet. I moved here, I started over, because I'd had enough curiosity, gossip, and rumors for three lifetimes.''

Paige sucked in a breath, remembering what Clay had said about the grapevine in Langley.

"Did you know anybody when you moved here?'' Ben seemed to have one question after another and was asking them all. She hated to see Clay go through the inquisition, but this was the purpose behind his visit—to give Ben insight.

Clay answered Ben without hesitating. "No one. And I thanked God for that.'' He ran his hand over his face. "Do you get what I'm telling you, Ben? You lost the dream of football. I lost my whole life. Do you think I never wanted to quit? Do you think I didn't want to hole up in my room, brooding about life's unfairness? I can remember not wanting a future. Not caring at times if I had one.''

Ben looked puzzled. "So what made you keep going?''

"My sister, my mother, the drive inside me that wouldn't let me give up.''

Ben dropped his head to his chest. "I don't know if I'm as strong as you are.''

Clay took a few steps closer to Ben's chair. "Look at me, Ben.''

The teenager brought his eyes to Clay's.

"You're as strong as you want to be. You've come this far, you have people who care about you, and you have no one peeking in the window to see how you're doing.''

Along with lightning and thunder, rain spattered the windows at first lightly, then with steady force. For the moment, it was the only sound in the room.

Paige could see that the last half hour had been rough on Clay. His expression was strained, his hands tightly closed. She hadn't had enough time to absorb it all yet, but one emotion pushed against all the others. Hurt.

Why hadn't Clay trusted her enough to confide in her? Had he been afraid she'd go spread his story across Langley? He'd said as much once. His lack of trust hurt, mostly because she'd had to find out like this, not when they were alone. If it weren't for Ben, would Clay ever have told her about the amnesia? Could love grow when there was no trust?

Ben looked at Paige, then back at Clay. "So what you guys are saying is that I should get a life."

Paige tore her thoughts from Clay and concentrated on Ben. "You can't isolate yourself from the world. You have to envision what you want and go after it."

Clay added, "If you want to date, you have to ask girls for dates. And if you want a successful future, you have to do what you can to get it. Can you honestly see yourself pumping gas or working at a sporting goods store the rest of your life? Is that enough of a challenge?"

"*You* work in a store."

Clay gave a wry smile. "Score one for you. But I also own the store. I do the PR work, the managing, the repairs. I'm my own boss."

"I don't know what I want," Ben muttered.

Paige rose and went to the aquarium. She was taking a stab in the dark, but it was one worth taking. "Did you set this up?"

"Yeah. I have three more up in my room. One saltwater, two freshwater."

"This is beautiful, Ben. I heard they're not easy to get started or keep."

He shrugged. "It just takes time. There has to be the right filtration to meet the demands of the fish."

She smiled at his technical use of the language that had come out so easily. "Your counselor told me you show a high aptitude in science."

"I do this for fun. I like to read about marine biology, coral reefs. I guess that's why."

Clay picked up on Paige's idea. "Work should be something you like to do, something that interests you."

There was a different light in Ben's eyes as he studied the aquarium pensively. "The counselor mentioned studying biology, but I don't know."

Clay nodded. "Think about it. Think about what you want to be doing five years from now, ten years from now."

Ben mumbled, "Maybe I can look over some of the college brochures."

The lights flickered again as the wind whooshed and rain beat against the house.

Clay's eyes were shadowed as he looked at Paige. "We'd better get going."

A flash of lightning illuminated the sky, a crack sounded, the lights went out as sirens blew.

Ben's mother came into the living room with a flashlight. "You're welcome to stay until the electricity comes back on."

Paige could see only Clay's shadow, tall and broad by Ben's chair. She couldn't see his face, but she could feel his coiled energy and wasn't surprised by his answer.

"Paige, if you're game, I'd rather leave. Shep won't be happy with the lights out and the thunder booming."

She was fairly certain Clay was more agitated than Shep right now. He wanted to go home—to a home where he could withdraw from a nosy world. She suspected he'd said everything he had to say, everything he could say, and if he stayed, he might have to answer questions that brought back more turmoil and pain.

Even driving in a storm, she could trust Clay, despite the fact he didn't seem able to trust her. "We can leave now. If we wait, the streets could flood."

Mrs. Hockensmith went to the hall closet and felt for

something along the side. "I only have this golf umbrella, but it's better than nothing."

Ben said softly, "Mr. Reynolds, I can bring the trophies by your house sometime. I'd like to look at them again if you don't mind."

Clay's answer was gruff. "I don't mind." He took the umbrella and waited for Paige by the door.

Paige touched Ben's shoulder. "Think about what Clay said."

She saw him nod.

Clay went out on the porch and opened the umbrella. Paige took his arm so she could stay close to him. It was stiff, as tense as he was. The umbrella didn't do much good. The wind slapped them with rain as they ran to the Blazer. Clay opened the passenger's door, holding the umbrella as she climbed in. She didn't even have time to say thank you as he slammed the door shut and hurried to the driver's side.

Tossing the umbrella into the backseat, he shook the raindrops from his arm. "We'll go to my place and see what the conditions are like before we attempt to go to Doc's."

"Doc's not home," she murmured. "He went to his sister's and is staying the night." Paige suspected Doc had left to give her time alone to think about Clay, her mother, and Africa.

Clay started the engine and switched on the headlights. As they drove down rain-drenched streets, Paige remembered a similar drive after their day at the amusement park. But they'd arrived home at the *end* of the storm. This one was just beginning.

Their headlights and the flashes of lightning were the only illumination. The roads looked eerie with the street-lights dark, no lamps blazing in the houses they passed. The wind swept tree branches across the streets. As Clay headed out of the residential section, a cluster of branches suddenly flew at Paige's side of the windshield. She gasped.

Clay swore. Then he muttered, "We'll be home soon."

Instead of being comforting, his words made Paige's stomach flip-flop. And what would happen once they were there alone? Would he talk to her? Would he tell her what he was feeling? Or would he hold on to his silence for protection and, as soon as the storm subsided, take her back to Doc's?

She studied him in the shadows. His body was rigid, his broad shoulders held stiff as he looked straight ahead. From the glow of the dashboard, she could see both of his hands tightly enclosing the wheel. She wondered if he ever let his guard down, if he could ever truly relax. From the sounds of it, that happened only with Trish and his mother.

No past. Lord, Paige couldn't imagine how to handle that. To think back and have . . . nothing. Yet again, maybe that's where Clay got his forward-looking attitude. There *was* no looking back. That's why he could play and work and thoroughly enjoy himself. Except where she was concerned.

The question again came back to haunt her. Why couldn't he trust her? Had something else happened that Clay hadn't told Ben? What about the woman Doc had mentioned? Where did she fit in? And what about Clay's father?

Paige had so many questions. But she couldn't ask them. Clay had to open up to her on his own.

The heavy rain quickly raised puddles. Some covered half the road. When the night shrouded one pool until Clay was on top of it, the Blazer sloshed through the water. She heard Clay's sigh of relief when the engine didn't stall out.

A few minutes later, he turned down the lane and parked next to the front walk. "This is one time when I wish I'd built a garage."

"I won't melt," Paige commented.

Clay turned off the windshield wipers and headlights and they sat in the darkness. Paige had never felt closer to Clay, yet so far away. The rain closed them in. She could smell the faint trace of Clay's shampoo, see his large shadowy outline, hear his breathing. She waited for him to say something that would open a door between them.

All he said was, "Let's get out of this."

Her hand trembled as she reached for the buckle on her seat belt. The catch wouldn't open.

He undid his belt and heard her fumbling with hers. "Problems?"

Her voice seemed to desert her as the emotions from the evening gathered in her throat.

His hand covered hers. "Let me."

While she soaked in his warmth, the comfort of his touch, he asked, "Paige?"

She pulled her hand away so he could help.

He pressed the button and the seat belt retracted. So did Clay as he moved away from her and opened his door. "Stay put," he commanded.

Grabbing the umbrella, he jumped out and came around to open her door.

Paige didn't touch him as they hurried to the front porch under the umbrella. She couldn't see his face as he closed the material and leaned the handle against the house. Shep began barking as Clay dug in his pocket for the key.

He opened the door and Shep stopped barking. Clay let Paige precede him inside. She stood in the darkness as Shep rubbed his head against her leg.

Clay went to the kitchen. "I'll get a flashlight and some candles."

She heard him open a closet, pull open a drawer. A cupboard closed. Metal clanked against metal. She saw a small glow of light. Careful not to run into furniture in the dark living room, she went to the kitchen.

She watched Clay, as by the light of a flashlight he trimmed the wick on a candle, put it in its old-fashioned holder, and lit it. He did the same with another.

"Can I do anything to help?"

He looked at her then. In the glow of the candle she saw his fatigue. She felt drained, too.

Lightning lit up the kitchen, and a moment later, thunder crashed. Wind and rain battered against the back walls.

"Paige, I don't really feel like going out in this again. My spare bedroom's made up for when Trish visits. How about if you just stay overnight?" When she hesitated, he said, "Doc's not home to worry about you."

She didn't know why she was hesitating. She didn't want to go back outside any more than Clay. If she stayed the night, what? Maybe Clay would talk to her? He wasn't in a talking mood and she knew it. It hurt to be this close to him yet not close enough. Maybe in the morning when they were both rested . . .

He handed her the flashlight. "You'll stay?"

She took it from him. "Yes."

"Trish keeps spare clothes in the dresser. Maybe she left pajamas or something. I'll lead the way with the flashlight if you want to bring one of the candles. I think I have another flashlight in the closet upstairs."

Clay wasn't just keeping his distance emotionally, but physically, too.

She followed him up the stairs, her hand cupped around the candle flame so it didn't blow out. He led her into a room a bit smaller than the master bedroom into which she'd peeked before. It was difficult to see the decor in the shadows, but she could see a quilt on the double bed. Colored patches made up large rings that intertwined. She guessed the cannonball headboard was dark pine.

Clay went to the dresser and pulled open the top drawer. The first item he pulled out was a pastel cotton and lace shift. His gaze met hers, and even without electric lights, she could see sparks of desire in his eyes as he looked at it, then looked back at her.

She knew he was imagining her in the short nightdress. He knew she knew.

Clay stuffed it back in the drawer and said gruffly, "Look through everything and find what you want. Trish won't mind. I'll go check on the other flashlight."

He was gone before she could open her mouth.

Paige sifted through the drawer and decided the cotton would be the most practical. As soon as the storm stopped, she'd probably have to open the windows so the room didn't become stifling.

Clay was back in a few moments. He laid a second flashlight on the nightstand.

"Are you going to bed now?" Paige asked tentatively.

"As soon as the thunder dies down, I'll let Shep out. He'll probably make it a quick trip with the rain. So if you want to use the bathroom first, go ahead. There are some magazines under the nightstand if you want to try to read by candle or flashlight. They're Trish's, so I don't know what's there."

Clay was making it clear they weren't talking about anything tonight. He couldn't wait to get out of the room.

He ran his hand through his hair. "I'll try to find an extra toothbrush and lay it on the sink."

Paige took a few steps closer to him. She had to give him an opening if he wanted it. "Clay, what you did tonight for Ben was important."

He searched her face. "I hope so." Then he headed for the door. "I'll see you in the morning."

Paige nodded.

Clay stepped into the hall and closed her door. He rolled his head and shrugged his shoulders to try to release the tension. The brief stretching didn't work. He was wound tight.

It had taken every ounce of control he possessed to

leave that room, not to ask Paige what she thought, not to ask her how she felt, not to take her in his arms. But beyond the beauty of her face glowing in the candle-light, beyond the confusion on her face when she looked at him, one question burned too fiercely for him to ignore.

Had he unleashed a force tonight that could destroy his life again?

ELEVEN

Black. Black everywhere. Freezing cold as he'd never known it. Clashing colors colliding—purple, red, orange. Emptiness. In his mind he reached for something, anything, and couldn't find it. He ran and ran and ran. His head pounded, his heart felt as if it would burst. Pain, sharp and stabbing, pulsed from his temples to his toes. But he kept running.

A white jagged wall rose in front of him. He changed direction only to be met by another, and another. Walls in all directions. Walls, steep and treacherous, with no handholds or footholds. But he couldn't stop running.

He put out his hands in front of him. Maybe he could charge through. Maybe the walls were illusions. He had to take the chance. He couldn't keep running, he couldn't keep turning around.

He plunged ahead and the wall moved away from him. He couldn't reach it. The faster he ran, the faster it moved. He turned in another direction. That wall did the same thing. Now he couldn't get close to it.

Icy moisture dripped down his forehead, his arms. Beyond the walls lay release. If he could get past them, he could find peace.

He stopped running and stood as still as the silence. The walls stopped moving. His body pounded with fierce pain, but he couldn't tell where it was coming from. He looked to the left and the right and saw nothing but white ice piercing the black vacuum.

The freezing cold penetrated his fingers, his face, his legs, his chest. It should have brought relief, numbness, but it brought fiery burning instead. Maybe if he could move, maybe if he could run again, he could escape it.

He tried to lift his foot. It was frozen in place. He tried to lift his hand. It was a dead weight. No feeling, no sensation but the cold.

His mouth. He could feel his lips. He called for help. No one answered. He called again. No one came. He was alone.

A fist jabbed at his stomach, pounded at his chest. It created a swirling of fear and panic. The fear and panic spun like a whirlwind inside him until he couldn't catch his breath. The walls, a few minutes before so far out of reach, began moving closer. The wall in front of him inched nearer and nearer, exuding an icy aura. He glanced to his right side. That wall was closing in, too. He looked over his shoulder just as he felt a blast of icy air at his back.

His left. Maybe he could escape to the left!

No. Freezing white rocks glided toward him.

Flashing colors again. He was trapped. There was no way out. Fear became the enemy, panic became its twin. He couldn't see, he couldn't hear, he couldn't breathe. With a last-ditch monumental surge of hope, he called out. . . .

"Clay! Clay, it's Paige. Look at me."

He felt the sweat dripping from his brow, the icy numbness fading. No white walls, no rocks. The sheets were tangled around his legs as if he'd been rolling in them. As Paige's concerned blue eyes searched his face, his heaving breaths became more regular. Until he realized Paige was sitting on the side of his bed in a nightgown. As panic and fear ebbed away, something stronger and more potent made his breathing become labored again.

"Go back to your room, Paige."

She didn't move. "Tell me about it, Clay. Tell me what's tearing you up. Let somebody in."

She was seeing him at his most vulnerable. The nightmares always shook his life and, for those dream-filled minutes, he was out of control. He hated the feeling. He hated Paige's seeing him like this. "It was a nightmare. A result of the accident. It has nothing to do with you."

She laid the flashlight on the nightstand, reached out, and stroked his jaw. "You don't have to go through this alone."

Her touch was fire. It rushed through him like a brush blaze caught by the wind. He didn't want to fight the passion anymore. He didn't want to fight her.

The soft cotton shift lay gently over her breasts. One shoulder tipped over her arm. Her blue eyes were huge, wide, soft, so inviting. As he stared, she parted her lips slightly, and he realized the small gasp was in response to his perusal. Heavy desire pulsed through him, making his need more insistent than logic. He knew his limits.

He took her hand from his cheek and held it away from him. "If you don't want something to happen you'll regret later, leave now."

She didn't flinch from the raspy desire in his voice or the compelling intensity of his gaze. "I won't regret it."

Clay couldn't keep his hands from framing Paige's face. He couldn't keep from leaning toward her, pulling her toward him. He couldn't keep from needing her, wanting her, or hoping this wasn't all wrong. His mouth came down on hers forcefully. He invaded her feminine softness with no attempt at gentleness or finesse. Maybe he wanted to see how she'd react. Maybe he wanted to see if she needed him the same raw way he needed her. If she didn't, he wanted to scare her away.

Paige's moan vibrated through Clay. She didn't shy away from his tongue but met him stroke for stroke as if a dam had burst inside her, too.

He never thought a kiss could be this intimate. He ran his hands over her face, memorizing the exquisite softness, the silk of her brows, the ridge of her cheekbones, the delicate slant of her jaw, her small chin. He splayed his hands through her hair and pulled her toward him as he lay on the pillow.

She curled into him.

He tore his lips from hers to make sure one last time. "Paige, are you certain you want to do this?"

"Yes."

All barriers were gone. Clay was going to accept what she offered and satisfy them both. His passion for her took over. He turned on his side and filled his senses with her. He smelled Paige and roses. He closed her in his embrace until every available inch of his body touched every available inch of hers. He revelled in having Paige this close, and he shook with the intensity of his emotions.

He pulled away from their kiss, but she protested with a small moan. She kissed his chin, his cheek, then returned to his lips. He could feel her body trembling, too. She was so damn responsive. The tip of her tongue played with his upper lip.

He yanked her gown up to her waist. He didn't want cotton in his hands, he wanted her. When he caressed her hip, she arched toward him. "Paige, do you know what you're doing to me?"

He thought she shook her head, but he couldn't tell. "Sit up, Paige."

She gazed at him with blue eyes alive with desire. "Why?"

"Because I want to touch *you*, not this damn gown."

She sat up and he lifted it over her head. She was naked to his gaze, perfect, beautiful. "Looking at you takes my breath away."

She smiled shyly.

He stripped off his jogging shorts and bent to kiss her again. The honest desire between them intoxicated him. He kissed her neck, pausing at the base of her throat.

She wove her hands into his hair.

Clay stroked her shoulders and rubbed his chin along the upper moon of her breast. She writhed under him. When he rasped his beard over her nipple, she gave a small cry.

"I want you, Paige. I'm crazy with wanting you."

Her fingers kneaded his scalp. "I want you, too. Make love to me, Clay."

She'd asked him once before and he'd pushed her away. He couldn't do that now. She was a balm for his heart, the match to his desire, and, right now, an antidote for his dreams. The nightmares made him feel powerless; she made him feel strong.

A surge of desire he couldn't control brought his lips to hers. He bit her lower lip and she arched against him, almost sending him over the edge. She curved into him, her nails raking his shoulders. He ravaged her mouth.

He moved to her breast and flicked his tongue over the aroused nipple. She called his name. It added fuel to the consuming blaze.

Paige couldn't control how she felt, how her body was responding, the love overriding the passion.

She scraped her nails down the curve of Clay's spine. His ministration to her nipple pulled deep inside her. The tingles throughout her body, the tension tightening her womanly center promised something wonderful. She loved the feel of Clay, his heat, every different texture from his chest hair to the velvet softness of his manhood that scorched and throbbed against her thigh.

She'd never done this before, but she suspected what would give him as much pleasure as he was giving her. She reached down and curled her hand around him. He took sharp breaths, then plunged his tongue into her mouth again and again, deeper and deeper.

She'd never experienced the coiling passion that could draw her body toward one erotic sensation. She'd never experienced this need to have her body completed by a man. But not just any man—Clay.

She caressed him until he tore his mouth from hers and rose above her. She felt his hand between her thighs and realized even in the throes of passion that he was thinking of her, making sure she was ready for him. She should tell him. . . .

But she didn't have a chance.

He thrust into her with a strong, slick stroke. She didn't cry out, but clenched his arms with the sudden sharp pain.

He stilled and stared down at her with the recognition of what had just happened. "Dammit, Paige, why didn't you tell me? Why didn't you stop me?"

He began to withdraw.

She wrapped her legs around him, knowing she needed him inside her more than she needed petting, gentleness, or Clay changing his mind. For this moment, he was hers and she was his. Nothing . . . absolutely nothing would change that.

She arched up, taking him deeper.

His voice was thick, torn from his throat. "Paige, I won't be able to stop."

"Don't stop. Show me. Take me with you. I want this, Clay. I want you."

She felt his shudder of acceptance, the tension in his corded muscles that told her he was going to make this good for her if it killed him.

She took him as deep as she could, forgetting about the slash of pain as soon as he began moving inside her. He was hot and hard, and strong, and filled with life. She needed all of that. Soon, the wonderful, novel sensations overtook conscious thought. Each stroke excited her, lifted her, joined her with Clay in a way nothing else could.

She shimmered with the excitement, shivered from the power, shook from the pleasure, and held on for dear life.

She felt her woman's center pulse around him, contract, tighten, clasp him with love. She thought she couldn't know any more pleasure, any more closeness, until Clay shifted, brought his hand between them, and touched her so intimately she almost arched off the bed.

The flood of sparkling, glorious sensations washed over her again and again and again. "Clay, it's so wonderful. Don't stop!"

He didn't. With each thrust, she gasped and held him, glorying in the ecstasy.

Clay propped his hands on either side of her shoulders, kissed her with an intensity that took her above the clouds, above the moon, above the stars. His strokes were slow and rhythmic until neither of them could control the pace turning frenzied and wild.

Then Clay shuddered, stilled, shuddered, and shuddered again.

Paige had fallen asleep in Clay's arms. But Clay didn't sleep, wouldn't sleep. He couldn't take the chance the nightmare would return. Not when Paige was with him like this.

Like this.

It never should have happened. She was a virgin! *Had* been a virgin. He should have known. He should have guessed. There'd been signs all along the way. She wasn't world-wise. She wasn't man-wise. He'd mistaken honest passion for experience.

What he regretted most was the way it had happened. He'd felt panicked, vulnerable, and he was afraid he'd used Paige as an escape. That wasn't fair to her. And if he'd known she was a virgin . . .

The first time should have been special, slow, easy, lingering. It should have been music and flowers and wine.

He would have been careful with her, arousing her to such a high pitch she wouldn't have noticed the pain.

He should have stopped. He should have . . .

Paige stirred against him. She snuggled deeper into his shoulder, moved her fingers over his chest. She was breathing deeply and he knew the movements were involuntary. But they aroused him. And he wanted her all over again.

Okay, he'd told her about the amnesia and she hadn't run in the opposite direction. He'd seen the shock on her face, but he wasn't sure what it meant. He'd felt too raw last night, too emotionally spent to discuss it. So he didn't know how she really felt.

Just because she'd made love with him . . . He closed his eyes tight. He knew better than anyone how compassionate Paige could be. If that was why she'd come to him, if that was why she'd let him pull her into his bed, he had even more reason to regret last night, to regret Paige becoming an important part of his life.

Paige turned over, reached for the warmth she'd known all night, but found only a cool sheet. She opened her eyes and squinted against the bright sunlight shining in the open window.

Clay stood there in his gray jogging shorts, looking out. His hand was propped high on the window frame. The scars crisscrossed his shoulder. She remembered the feel of them under her fingers. She remembered the feel of him inside her. She smiled. Making love was much more extraordinary than all her clinical knowledge had led her to expect.

Clay must have felt her gaze on him. He turned toward her, the sun shimmering in the few strands of gray in his hair. The expression on his face was studiously neutral. Much too neutral.

Her smile faded away and she propped on her elbow. "How long have you been awake?" she asked, not knowing how to act the morning after, suspecting Clay didn't share her fulfillment or happiness.

"All night."

His bare chest, his wide shoulders were a distraction. "But every time I woke, you were holding me." She wished he was holding her now.

"I wasn't up. I was awake."

"Why?"

He faced her squarely then and leaned against the windowsill. "I didn't want to invite another nightmare."

"How often do you get them?"

"They stopped over a year ago. They started again the day we took Ben to the lake." His answer was dispassionate, as if it didn't matter.

"Oh, Clay."

His voice was harsh. "I don't want your pity."

Suddenly she knew exactly what he was thinking, why he was so removed. "You think last night was about pity?" She sat up and crossed her legs Indian fashion under the sheet.

"I was shaken up after the nightmare."

"And you didn't know what you were doing?"

He scowled. "I knew exactly what I was doing."

She straightened her shoulders. "Good. Because so did I. And pity didn't enter into it."

His green eyes grew darker. "Don't tell me you didn't feel sorry for me."

"Sorry? The only thing I'm sorry about is that you couldn't trust me enough to tell me about the amnesia before last night. How do you think I felt hearing about it at Ben's? Why couldn't you trust me, Clay? Why?" She hadn't intended to throw all that at him now, but she had to know.

He was silent and she thought he might not answer. But then he said, "Because I've been in this situation before. People don't look at amnesia like a cold or the flu, Paige.

They don't look at it in the same way as a lost arm or leg. They see it as a deficiency.''

He was generalizing and lumping her in with everyone else. That hurt. ''We're not talking about *some* people. We're talking about *me*. Why couldn't you trust *me?*''

''My father still doesn't accept it.''

His father might be part of it, but not all of it. ''And who else?''

There was that look again, as if Clay wanted to pull her close and push her away at the same time. ''I dated a woman a couple of years ago.''

''You told her about the amnesia?''

Clay didn't look at Paige, but at the wall behind her. ''One night she stayed; I had a nightmare. I'd gone a few months without one, so I thought it would be all right if she spent the night. But it wasn't. The nightmare was a bad one. I don't know how long it went on. She was scared out of her wits. I can't blame her. If that happened to a woman when I was with her—''

''You would hold her in your arms until the nightmare passed.''

Her sureness brought his gaze back to hers. ''It's different for men and women.''

Paige arched her brows. ''I don't see why.''

He let that basis for argument pass. ''After I came out of it, I explained about the amnesia.''

''And?''

He sighed. ''She tried to accept it.''

''What do you mean she tried?'' If the woman loved Clay, accepting his past or a lack of one shouldn't have mattered.

''She pretended it didn't matter.''

''How do you know it didn't?''

He thought about it for a moment. ''She'd give me these odd looks when she thought I didn't notice. And she treated me differently.''

''Like?''

"Like I wasn't all there. Like I was less than I was before. It was a . . . solicitous attitude, as you'd have with a child. And she wouldn't stay overnight. She told me outright she couldn't contend with the nightmares. So the relationship crumbled. We weren't equals anymore. Everything was different. Neither of us wanted it to be, but we couldn't help it."

"What was her name?"

He seemed surprised that she asked. "Clare."

Paige sat up straighter in the bed. "I'm not Clare."

He studied her carefully. She could feel his eyes on her face, her bare shoulders. "No, you're not. But this time its worse. Can't you see I used you last night for an escape? I needed to feel strong, in control of something." He gave a bitter laugh. "Some kind of control. I hadn't been with a woman in two years. Just how do you think I feel this morning, Paige, knowing I took advantage of you?"

All of the emotion inside her, her love for Clay, her frustration with him, exploded. "You're absolutely impossible!" She threw her legs over the side of the bed and hopped up. "If you think Ben Hockensmith is stubborn and can't see the forest for the trees, go look in your mirror. I may have been a virgin, Clay, but I'm not stupid and I have a will of my own. I climbed into bed with you last night, I kissed you, I made love with you because that's what *I* wanted." She crossed to the door. "When you clear your head of misguided chivalry, maybe we can talk as *equals*."

Until she met Clay, Paige had never realized just how angry she could get with a person. She'd always gotten angry at circumstances, governments, man's inability to help his fellow man. Maybe she'd never gotten this angry with anyone because she'd never cared about anyone the way she cared about Clay. She wasn't sure who he was trying to protect, himself or her.

She dressed. As she went down the hall, she saw Clay's bedroom door standing open. Going downstairs, she wasn't surprised when she peered out the kitchen window and saw him in the backyard with Shep. She took a long look. He'd put on a pale blue T-shirt, but she remembered the powerful shoulders underneath. His jogging shorts emphasized the strength of his thighs, the length of his legs. She remembered them intertwined with hers. She would *not* regret last night even if Clay did.

She pulled a pitcher of orange juice from the refrigerator and was pouring herself a glass when Clay came back in. Shep trotted over to her, waited for her to scratch between his ears, then went to his food dish.

Paige was afraid to look at Clay, to have him deny again what last night had meant. So she concentrated on her glass of juice. "I didn't know if you wanted me to start breakfast or if you'd want to take me back to Doc's right away."

"I don't want to take you back to Doc's."

His gravelly tone made her meet his gaze.

He approached her slowly. "I'm sorry I didn't tell you about the amnesia before we went to Ben's. I thought it would be easier on both of us to let it come out the way it did, but I can see now that it wasn't."

Clay was close enough to touch. But *she* didn't want to regret whatever happened next. "If it hadn't been for Ben, would you have told me?"

"I was coming to that decision. Ben's situation just pushed it a little."

She believed him, not just because she wanted to but because she knew Clay wouldn't lie to her. "I want to understand, Clay. About everything."

He reached out and caressed her cheek. "I know you do. But that might take some time—time we don't have if you go back to Africa."

She was purposely *not* thinking about Africa. She'd

have to do that soon enough. "We can use the time we do have."

He rubbed his thumb across her chin. "I'm sorry about last night, too." When she opened her mouth to protest, he laid his fingers over her lips. "It should have been special for you. Not so . . . fast."

"It was special. For *me*."

He must have seen the misgiving in her eyes, her worry that last night had been just a release for him, nothing more.

He pulled her into his chest, against his heart. "I've never known anything like last night, Paige, and I guess because of that, I tried to make it less than it was."

She leaned back and saw the vulnerability in his eyes. He still doubted she could accept his amnesia. "*If* we had last night to do over again, what would you do differently?"

"I'd tell you about the amnesia, I'd give you time to think about it, and then if you were still here, I'd make slow, tender love to you."

His husky voice, the underlying passion, made her tremble. "I don't need time to think about it and I'm still here."

His low groan was one of surrender to his desire for her, to the feelings between them. His beard stubble grazed her as he lay his cheek against hers, the gesture almost more intimate than a kiss. He rubbed sensually back and forth, creating the desire for more than cheek touching cheek.

But he'd said he wanted to give her slow and lingering last night, and that's clearly what he was going to give her now. He moved to her hair, rubbed his cheek at her temple, and took a slow, deep breath.

"Clay?"

"You always smell like roses. I can't seem to breathe you in deep enough to make it last, to make me remember always."

"That's important to you."

"Every new memory is important. It has to do double duty for one I can't get back."

Strong emotions shook her voice, her sorrow over Clay's loss, the love she wanted to share with him. "I want to make lots of memories with you."

His arms brought her tighter against him. His jogging pants were soft, almost nonexistent against her cotton slacks. She could feel his arousal pressing hot and hard against her. He wanted her and she gloried in that, afraid to wonder what type of feelings were attached to the wanting. Her own feelings were too rare, too precious to try to analyze them.

Clay whispered her name and she just held him, held on to the moment, making it an indelible memory—the tenderness, the gentleness, the passion shaking both of them.

It was almost more than she could absorb: Clay's hard heat, the gentle whisper of his lips on her forehead, her eyelids, her nose . . . and finally when she didn't think she could stand the waiting . . . her mouth.

He pecked and nipped at her until she tightened her arms around his neck and parted her lips. Still, he played with such sweetness, such slow tenderness, she wanted to beg him for more. But there were no words, only feelings. She touched the corner of his lips with her tongue and felt him shudder.

"Do you try to drive me wild, or does it come naturally?" he murmured.

"It must come naturally," she managed. "I'm not trying to do anything but get you to kiss me."

He chuckled and leaned away. "I *am* kissing you."

She blushed. "You know what I mean."

He laughed and locked his hands behind her back. "You have the loveliest blush."

"I can't seem to control it when I'm around you."

"Don't try." He bent his head and took her lower lip between his teeth.

She softly sighed. There was no way she was going to rush him, and deep down she knew she didn't want to try. She wanted each and every nuance of passion with Clay, because it might have to last her a lifetime.

Clay kissed her neck and sucked on her earlobe until her knees gave. He swung her into his arms and carried her to his bedroom.

Last night had been shrouded in shadows. The flashlight on Clay's nightstand was a reminder of the storm. This morning was alive with light. The sun streaked across his bed, the summer's morning breeze swished past the raised venetian blinds. Birds chirped to each other, one singing a louder song than his friends.

Clay sat down on the bed with her on his lap. His green eyes told her things his heart couldn't yet find the words for. He kissed her then, the kind of kiss she wanted. She opened her lips and he took her with deep primitive strokes she returned in full measure. Each stroke of her tongue on his told him she wanted last night repeated and he could speed up the process as much as he wanted.

He broke away, breathing hard and fast, and rested his forehead against hers. "You kiss like there's no tomorrow."

She tried to break through the daze of being kissed by Clay. "Sometimes there isn't."

"I only have tomorrows, Paige."

She knew what he meant. He didn't have a lifetime of yesterdays. But he didn't need them. Not now. "We have today."

He smiled. "Yes, we do. And we're going to make it last." Her expression must have been slightly dismayed because he said, "I'm going to teach you how exciting slow, long passion can be."

She put her hand on his chest. "I want to touch you."

He covered her hand with his, brought it to his lips, and kissed her palm. "You can touch me all you want."

She pulled up his T-shirt slowly, watching his face.

"You take a guy at his word."

"I take *you* at your word." She slipped her hand under the soft blue cotton, loving his warmth, his chest hair against her fingers. She wanted to taste his chest, rub her cheek against it. . . . The deep pulling inside her tugged tighter. There might be some merit in this "slow" idea.

She asked shyly, "Can we get undressed?"

He grinned. "That's definitely part of the plan."

Something was different about Clay, freer. She hoped she could give him all the acceptance, all the love that he'd needed and hadn't received.

They watched each other undress, teasing with their eyes, teasing with their smiles. She'd felt more than seen Clay's body last night. Now, in the light of day, he was beautiful, his desire imposing, his need clear.

He flopped the pillows against the headboard, propped against one, and stretched out his hand to her. His gaze swept over her, every part of her, and she felt hot all over. Her hand trembled as she took his.

She fitted against him, almost afraid to explore all the new feelings. Fast was easier in a way. There were fewer insecurities and less knowing, but much less anticipation.

She rubbed her cheek against his nipple and felt him suck in a breath. "Feel good?"

He cupped her breast in his palm. "Very good." He ran his finger in a circle around her nipple. "How about this?"

She closed her eyes, absorbed in the sensation. "Very good."

"Don't close your eyes. Don't hide from me."

She opened them. When he circled her nipple again, she swallowed hard, kept her gaze on his, and probably blushed from her eyebrows to her toes.

"Lord, you're beautiful."

She felt the blush fade as she became more comfortable with her nakedness and Clay's.

She touched the pad of her forefinger to the top of his

erect nipple and watched his lids half close. But he gave her a slanted smile. She tasted him with her tongue then, swirling around his nipple, teasing the peak. When she looked up, the smile had disappeared.

His voice was a husky rasp. "I think slow's going down the drain."

She'd never realized that pleasuring Clay could be so arousing. She put her mouth on him again, tasting, twirling, tormenting. Clay's breathing became more shallow, less rhythmic. With her hip against his leg, she could feel his thigh tighten. She felt powerful and excited, and desire rushed through her faster than any heat or cold, faster than the speed of sound or light, faster than she could ever dream.

She lifted her head, lowered her gaze to the dark thatch of hair below his navel, saw his complete arousal, and without thought and giving into instinct, laid her cheek against it.

Clay gasped.

She jerked away. "Sorry."

He caressed her back with a long stroke. "Don't be sorry. But do it again and we might have to start all over."

"Clay, I don't know what I can and can't do. I don't know—"

"I know you don't. And I'm so glad."

Paige's innocence was driving Clay insane. He wanted to let her explore, to let her do anything and everything she wanted. But his desire for her was too fierce, too demanding. If he let her stroke him, it would be all over. This was about her pleasure, not his.

He'd made a decision this morning. He was tired of living on the fringe. He was going to take a chance on Paige, a chance on them. For as long as he could.

His blood pulsed in the erect flesh she'd so tenderly touched, but he ignored it, gently pulled her to him, and said, "Now it's your turn, Paige. This is going to be all for you."

TWELVE

A thought suddenly hit Paige, something she *should* have thought about last night. "Clay, I can't."

"What do you mean you can't?"

"*We* can't. I can't believe I'm a doctor and I just remembered . . ."

"Birth control." He opened the drawer in the nightstand and lifted out a handful of foil packets.

"Saving up for a rainy day?" she teased, not understanding. He'd said he hadn't been with a woman for two years.

"Saving up for you." He stroked her hair away from her face. "I'm sorry I got carried away last night and didn't think about it. You know if anything happens, I'll stand by you."

If anything happened . . . A baby. Her baby and Clay's. The decision about Africa would be made for her. She'd never jeopardize a child's well-being. She did some quick calculation and in a way felt disappointed.

"It was my safe time, Clay. I don't think we have to worry." Did she see the same flicker of disappointment in his eyes that she felt?

If she did, it was soon replaced by a flicker of another

kind. He laid the packets on the nightstand and shook his head. "I went to Westminster to buy these. I knew if I bought something like that in Langley, rumors would fly all over town."

"That would bother you? To have people know we're . . . together?" She didn't know quite how to phrase it.

"Wouldn't it bother you?"

Living and traveling the way she had, seeing different mores in various cultures, she had never lived by anyone else's accepted idea of propriety. Gossip had never been an issue or a concern. She shrugged. "I don't know. I don't want to hide being together."

Clay's voice was low, his expression serious. "We don't have to hide, but I don't want people gossiping about my private life, either."

"Why did you come to a town like Langley if you didn't want the small-town curiosity?"

"I wanted the small-town friendliness."

She could understand how important that friendliness had been when he'd felt alienated from people in his past. But friendliness often brought curiosity. "The two sometimes go hand in hand."

"Maybe they do. But I'm not going to invite the curiosity." He shrugged off the seriousness and smiled. "*I'm* curious right now about . . ." He kissed her neck. "Whether you'd rather be kissed here . . ." He kissed just above her breast. "Or here."

The sensuous feel of his lips brought a sigh. He could melt her with a lot less. "Anywhere's fine."

"God, woman," he growled. "You know just the thing to say."

Her heart fluttered and she took refuge in honesty. "But not exactly what to do."

"You do everything just fine."

He brushed his lips across hers slightly once, twice. She clasped his shoulders to pull him to her. He kissed the tip of her nose. "Uh-uh. Not this time. You're not going to hurry me."

"Don't you want me to touch you, to hold you?"

"Oh, yes. But not too soon. Not yet." He took one of her hands, laced his fingers with hers, and held it above her shoulder. Then he took her other hand and drew her forefinger into his mouth.

First she felt a prick of beard, then the hot firmness of his lips. When his tongue swirled the tip of her finger, she released a small puff of air from the intense pleasure he was delivering. He sucked on her finger until she was breathing fast and moving restively against the sheet.

Smiling, he eased onto her body slowly, settling between her legs.

"Oh, Clay."

"What, Paige?"

"I feel so hot."

"And getting hotter," he murmured as he placed a kiss between her breasts.

Paige's breasts ached. She needed him to touch them, kiss them. But he didn't. He teased around them, driving her crazy. Heat gathered between her thighs, a heat like she'd never known.

She arched against him. Clay looked up, his eyes filled with green fire. His gaze moved from hers, to her lips, to her breasts, rosy with passion. The fire blazed brighter. She arched against him again and he swallowed hard.

"You're really trying to hurry me, aren't you?" he asked in a raspy voice.

"I ache for you, Clay. I want you inside me."

He took a deep breath and shook his head. "Patience, Paige."

"I have plenty of them," she mumbled.

He grinned and bent his head to her stomach. He kissed along her ribs while his hands sketched delicious patterns on her thighs. When he laved her navel, she threaded her fingers in his hair.

She felt soft, enticing pressure behind her legs and she shivered. He was urging her to raise her knees. She felt so vulnerable, so open, and suddenly she was scared.

His breath was warm on her skin, his expression was gentle. "Don't be afraid, Paige. I won't hurt you. I want to give you the pleasure you gave me last night. Trust me."

She moved her hands from his hair, down his strong neck. "I do."

His smile bathed her in safety, comfort, and promises.

He combed over the silky hair protecting the heart of her womanhood. Then he touched her layered softness reverently with exquisite tenderness. Tears came to her eyes and she blinked them away. The preciousness of Clay's touch melted her body and her heart. He explored farther into her heat and she moaned. Nothing in her entire life had ever prepared her for this.

She'd been alone for so long. It seemed she'd been lonely forever. She knew her parents loved her, but she'd been away from them so much. The friends she'd made at boarding school had temporarily pushed the loneliness away. Eventually, she'd poured all her passion, her heart, her soul into her patients and the science of healing. Work kept the loneliness sealed tightly in a corner of its own. But in Langley, loneliness had tapped her on the shoulder, reminding her it was still there. The child she couldn't save in Ethiopia had unsealed the box.

When Paige was with Clay, the loneliness dissolved. She felt connected to someone for the first time in her life.

Clay removed his hands from her, and she twisted to try to find them again.

"Easy, Paige. Easy." He stroked her inner thighs so lightly she thought she imagined it until her legs quivered and she shook all over. She opened her eyes to get Clay's reassurance.

He kept petting her, caressing her, watching her. He

was looking at her as if she was something beautiful, something to cherish. When he lowered his head, she closed her eyes.

The erotic satin of his tongue made her gasp and clutch the sheets. He touched, probed, teased until she rolled her head from one side to the other, saying his name over and over. He penetrated, withdrew, surrounded until an indescribable radiance focused at that one point. Swirl after swirl of pleasure tormented her until he finally enclosed the bud of her desire, bathed it in his tenderness, and Paige cried out.

She moaned as ecstasy swept her in a circle again and again, each spin around reaching deeper inside of her, ravaging her with pleasure, searing every part of her body.

And then finally she had Clay in her arms where she wanted him, where she needed him to be. He was inside her and she was complete.

She tried to speak but couldn't say anything that could nearly express the engulfing love, the fulfillment that Clay gave her. She moved her hips to take him deeper, and when she did, the pleasure overtook her again. She clung to him, giving in to elemental needs and fires that raged out of control.

The picnic had been Paige's idea. But instead of going to the lake, Clay had suggested they take their lunch to the clearing in the woods behind Doc's house. While Clay had scavenged in the refrigerator, Paige showered and changed into turquoise shorts and matching top. It clung to her soft curves, making Clay long to strip it off. But for now he just wanted to enjoy being with her.

Clay spread out their blanket on a patch of ground under a tall maple. He pulled out the turkey sandwiches he'd thrown together. "Hungry?"

Paige opened a bag of pretzels. "Starved." She smiled shyly. "I think we missed breakfast."

He laughed. "That depends on what kind of breakfast you wanted."

She blushed and he reached for her hand. Every time he looked at her now, every time she smiled or touched him, he thought about making love with her. He was sinking in, deeper and deeper, and he was letting it happen. What would he do if she left?

He did know, of course. He'd go on. Just as he had before. But this time the remembered loss would be far greater than any he had forgotten. He knew he should bring up the future. But he couldn't. Not today.

Glancing around, he released her hand and pushed himself to his feet.

"Where are you going?"

He tossed over his shoulder, "Be right back."

He went to the side of the sunny clearing and plucked flowers from the scattered beds. Black-eyed Susans, daylilies, bluets. It was a small variegated bouquet. Suddenly it didn't seem nearly enough. He should be ordering two-dozen long-stemmed roses for her to show her exactly how special she was. Maybe he should just put these aside.

But she was watching him, and he wanted to give her something. He took the flowers to her and laid them in her lap.

"They're lovely, Clay." She reverently touched a vibrant orange daylily.

He settled beside her. "I'd like to buy you a whole room of flowers. Last night meant a lot to me, Paige."

She brought a dainty bluet, a tiny four-petaled flower, to her nose and smelled it. "These mean more than anything you could buy."

He could see she meant it, and his heart opened to her even more. "You haven't asked me any questions."

She lay the flower back in her lap. "You'll tell me what you want me to know."

"I've told you a little bit of everything."

"Tell me about your dad," she requested softly, crossing her legs Indian fashion, cradling his flowers in her lap.

Paige's intuition shouldn't surprise him. She was a perceptive lady. Clay leaned back against the tree trunk. "If Mom and Trish had trouble accepting what happened to me, they worked through it. Mom made sure Trish talked to her, and they both saw a counselor for a while. What they were teaching me, the hours they spent with me would have been hard enough for professionals."

"They love you."

"I know. And I'll never be able to repay them for all they did. But my dad's an entirely different story."

"He didn't accept your amnesia as permanent?"

Clay realized she'd listened to everything he'd told Ben and filled in the gaps. "That was part of it. He couldn't believe the memories wouldn't return. He thought I wasn't trying hard enough. After a second doctor at a head-injury center confirmed the fact, Dad still wouldn't believe it. He wanted me to try hypnosis. And I did. But when something's wiped out, it's wiped out. I had this big blank bank and all I wanted to do was get on with filling it up."

"He couldn't let go of the past."

Clay drew one leg up and looked into the woods, wondering when thinking about his father would stop hurting. "Dad wanted back the son he knew. He wouldn't go to counseling with Mom and Trish. He didn't help in the reteaching process. And although no one would admit it, I could tell that he and Mom were pulling further apart. That's another reason I left Reisterstown. I figured with me gone, their lives could get back to normal."

"Have they?"

"I think so. That's the one thing Trish and I have never talked about. But Mom and Dad are still together."

"You felt responsible for all of it, didn't you?"

Clay's gaze met Paige's. "I *was* responsible."

"The accident was responsible."

Her blue eyes, her intent expression told him that was

so, but he grimaced. "It doesn't seem that simple when you're in the middle of it."

She nodded. "I know."

Paige was in the middle of a complicated situation now. The deeper they felt about each other, the more complicated it would get. Clay didn't want to waste any time they did have together. "I'd like you to meet Trish."

"I'd like that, too."

"Mom and Dad are giving her and her fiancé an engagement party. Would you like to go with me?"

"I'd like that very much."

He grinned. "You know what I'd like?"

"What?"

He took the wild flowers from her lap. Then he picked up one small bluet, the color of her eyes, and brushed it across her cheek. "I'd like to kiss you until nothing matters but the touch of our lips, the tangling of our tongues, me inside you."

She smiled, a soft sweet smile that wrenched his insides. "That would make me even happier than your gift of wild flowers."

He lay her down on the blanket, and as the summer sun dappled them with warmth, as the scent of green grass and trees and wild flowers wound about them, Clay kissed her and nothing else did matter.

Doc was sitting on the deck when Paige and Clay emerged from the woods after their picnic. Clay was sure Doc would know something had changed between himself and Paige. The older man didn't miss much.

Doc gave Clay a probing look, then grinned at Paige. She blushed prettily and took the picnic basket from Clay. "I'll put this away."

They hadn't made arrangements for the rest of the day, and Clay wanted to be with her. "Do you want to go to the lake this afternoon?"

"I usually spend Saturdays in the office working on

notes and updating files if there aren't any emergencies. But I think a day at the lake sounds much more therapeutic.''

When she smiled at him like that, he could forget where he was. It was going to be a *short* afternoon at the lake. His bedroom sounded like a much better idea.

She went into the kitchen and Doc commented, "She's much more relaxed than when she arrived." He looked at Clay. "I think you've had something to do with that."

"What do you think the chances are she'll stay?"

"Truthfully?"

Clay nodded.

"Even if she's thinking about it now, and realistically I don't know if she is, it will be a different cup of tea when her mother arrives."

"She's got to want what's best for Paige."

"Do *you* know what that is?" Doc's gaze was too penetrating, too knowing.

Clay looked out over the backyard. "I know what I want it to be."

Doc's voice brought Clay's gaze back to him. "I'm not sure Monica has ever really seen Paige as her daughter, but more as an appendage of herself. Charles and Monica's vision for their lives was so intense, Paige couldn't help but have it, too."

Clay ran his hand through his hair, more troubled by Doc's insight than he wanted to be. "So there's nothing I can do to help Paige with this."

"She has to make the decision on her own."

Anger rose in Clay. "With her mother pulling her *her* way."

"If you pull, too, Paige will be torn apart. She has to decide what she wants for her life, Clay. If you influence that and she makes the wrong decision, she'll resent it. She'll resent *you*."

The anger subsided and Clay shook his head. "Why is

it when I think I finally have a handhold on my life, I don't?"

A faint, wry smile touched Doc's lips. "Because life's constantly changing."

An idea had been forming in Clay's mind. "Do you think Paige would like to get dressed up and go someplace special?"

Doc grinned. "As in a *real* date?"

Clay grinned back. "Yeah. Women seem to like that sort of thing. It's just that Paige seems so different sometimes."

"I think she'd like it a lot." He stood. "Clay, if you're going to wage a campaign to get her to stay, you have about two weeks. Monica's due in around July first."

A campaign. Did he want to do that? He only knew he didn't want her to leave. "I'll keep that in mind."

Clay tugged at his tie as he walked to Doc's door the next Saturday evening. He hadn't worn a suit in at least a year. But he'd made reservations for dinner at a posh restaurant along the Chesapeake Bay. Paige's eyes had lit up like stars when he asked her to go dining and dancing with him.

The past week had seemed unreal in a way. He'd seen Paige almost every night. For propriety's sake she hadn't stayed overnight again and he didn't push it because he was still concerned about the nightmares. But after they made love, he'd wanted to keep her curled up next to him. Something seemed wrong about getting up, getting dressed, and going their separate ways.

He didn't have the chance to knock. Paige opened the door and his heart somersaulted. She'd swept the left side of her hair away from her face and clipped it with a pearl barrette. Her floral-patterned sundress was a natural bloom of colors in pink and lilac. The top fitted to her body perfectly while the knee-length skirt had three tiers. The neckline in front looked like the top of a heart.

She asked, "Would you like to come in for a few minutes?"

His mouth had gone dry. He cleared his throat. "No, I'm not sure how long it will take to get there. Are you ready?"

She lifted her small white purse. "All set."

She couldn't seem to take her eyes from him any easier than he could take his from her. Finally, she broke eye contact and turned the lock on the door before pulling it shut.

"Doc's not here?"

"He went to get a newspaper and a few groceries."

"He's almost back to full steam, isn't he?"

"He's doing well. He really doesn't need me here anymore."

Clay did. Yet how could he ask Paige to give up a dream when he didn't know if they had a future together? They needed time, just to be together. This was Paige's first serious relationship. He couldn't rush her into something she didn't want.

When Clay and Paige arrived at the restaurant, the maître d' asked if they would rather sit in the dining room or on the screened-in porch. They chose the porch.

Towering lights stood between trees at the back of the restaurant and cast their glow down levels of steps and a path along the bay. Clay could make out sparkling ripples under the moonlight.

Paige smiled. "This is lovely."

"*You're* lovely."

Her voice was husky. "You look different tonight."

"Different how?"

"I almost feel you're a stranger. You're very impressive in a suit and tie."

He took her hand and held it to his cheek. "I'm no stranger, Paige. I'm the same man you made love to last evening, the same man who wants you more each time he sees you."

"It's not just physical for you, is it, Clay?"

He couldn't say the words yet. Maybe because he wasn't ready to risk that much, maybe because he didn't want to pull her in two directions. But he could be honest. "No. It's not just physical."

The waitress came then with the wine list and he released Paige's hand.

Paige didn't know what she'd expected Clay to say. She certainly didn't want him to say something he didn't mean. What *if* he said he loved her? What would she do about it? Yes, she loved him. But she wasn't sure yet what that meant to her life. Her path had been mapped out for her since she was born. She'd never taken the reins herself to change direction because she thought she wanted what her parents wanted. Now she didn't know.

As she read over the menu, Clay asked, "What do you think? I've heard the chateaubriand's excellent. Is there anything you haven't tried before?"

She grinned. "The one without the price."

"Lobster? You've never had lobster? Then you haven't lived." He closed his menu. "We'll both have it."

"But you don't know how much—"

He took her hand. "There's no price limit on tonight, Paige. There's no limit at all."

The deep green of his eyes embraced her, and she felt as if she'd ascended to heaven.

Paige had tasted a multitude of foods ranging from snake to shark, both considered delicacies in some countries. She'd always tried to fit into her surroundings, to see the country through the eyes of its inhabitants. Tonight she wanted to see clearly, through her own eyes.

After the lobster arrived, she watched Clay dip a forkful into his melted butter. She did the same. The taste was sweet, tender, succulent.

Clay tilted his head and raised his brows as he waited for her verdict.

"It's wonderful."

His eyes twinkled then leapt with hot desire. "It can be even more wonderful." He took his fork, secured a small bite and dipped it into the butter. Then he held it in front of her.

She opened her mouth and he gently placed the fork on her tongue. Her gaze locked to his, she closed her lips, and he pulled the fork away. She savored the taste; she savored the intimacy.

Clay traced her bottom lip with his thumb, catching a drop of butter. He ran his thumb back and forth across her lip until she tingled to her fingertips. She licked her lips and his finger.

Passion flared brighter in his eyes. "Eating is supposed to satisfy hunger, not make it worse."

"It depends on what kind of eating you're doing." She picked up her knife and fork and cut off a piece of lobster. She dipped it in the butter and offered it to him.

He closed his lips around it and smiled.

Music wafted into the porch from the dining room. When they'd finished eating, Clay asked, "Would you like to dance?"

She wouldn't like anything more. At least she'd be closer to him, not a table length away.

Clay led her to the dance floor, his hand warm and protective on the small of her back. She felt safe when she was with Clay. And not just safe, but valued for who she was, not what she could do.

The ballad was perfect for a first dance. Clay guided her in the traditional box she'd learned at boarding school. But dancing with a man was much different than dancing with another fourteen-year-old.

Every once in a while Clay would embellish the box with a rocking step or a walking step that took them across the room. He'd warn her by the pressure of his hand on hers, a slight shifting of his palm on her back.

"When did you learn to dance?" She was eager to know everything about him. He'd told her what he'd learned from his family about his childhood, his college days. But she was much more interested in the years since the accident.

"About three years after the accident, I started dating again. Trish insisted dancing was a must-know. Much more important than ancient history."

Paige wanted to ask him something but wasn't sure how. "Am I different from other women you've known? I mean, I haven't had much experience and—"

Clay moved her hand from the classic position into his chest and held her tighter. "Yes, you're different. You're special. Experience sometimes makes a person hard. There's nothing hard about you, Paige. Or fake. You're naturally lovely, naturally soft, naturally sexy."

There was no doubt in the way he said it that he meant each and every word. She laid her head against his shoulder, appreciated the hard warmth of his body, his breath against her cheek, his lips nuzzling her neck. She couldn't think of a moment in her life that had ever been this happy.

As more couples crowded the small dance floor, Clay brought her closer. She wound her arms about his neck and pressed her lips to his throat. They were rocking to the music rather than dancing. But it didn't matter. She molded to Clay as if she were part of him, and maybe she was.

He didn't shift away from her or try to hide his arousal. He wanted her, and her heart danced its own free dance of joy. Clay kissed her temple, her cheek, the tender spot behind her ear. She trembled and held him tighter.

When the song ended, Clay gazed into her eyes. "Let's take a walk. I want to kiss you and this is a bit too public."

She smiled, kissed her forefinger, then touched it to his lips.

He shook his head and growled, "Actually I'd like to do a lot more than kiss you."

They returned to the porch and went out the back. Clay took Paige's elbow on the steps. They headed toward the path, and Clay held her hand as they walked. The smooth flow of the water was soundless. The slight breeze wafting over it gently lifted tendrils of Paige's hair and spread them across her cheek. She glanced at Clay as the breeze ruffled his hair, too. He looked pensive and didn't seem to notice.

She realized that since the first night they hadn't yet "slept" together in the true sense and guessed why. She said quietly, "I'd like to spend a whole night with you."

He knew exactly what she meant. "That might not be a good idea."

"Clay, I've seen your nightmare."

"No. You probably just caught the tail end. I don't want you around me when that happens."

"Why?"

He stopped walking. "I shouldn't have to spell it out. I'm not myself . . . I'm . . ."

"Vulnerable? There's nothing wrong with that. There's nothing wrong with needing someone to hold you. Why do you think there is?"

"Because when I have the nightmares, I feel helpless. I don't want you to see me like that."

"I would never think you're helpless. You're the strongest man I know. Just think about it, Clay, and know it won't make a difference between us, except maybe to bring us closer."

Clay surrounded her with his arms and brought her to him. When he bent his head, she lifted hers. Their lips met, caressed, held until he slid his tongue along her lower lip.

With an excited little moan, Paige opened her mouth to accept him. He didn't rush, taunting her with tiny flicks and quick forays. Soon she had enough of the teasing. Her hands held his head, and she gently caught his tongue between her teeth. There was no more playing.

Clay cupped her breasts as he delved deeper into her mouth. She rubbed against his hand wantonly. He tried to push the strap on her dress to the side, off her shoulder. But it wouldn't budge.

He broke the kiss and held Paige tight against his chest. "A kiss is never enough. I'd better take you home."

"I could get a few things together at Doc's and go home with you."

"I'm not ready for that yet, Paige. I had a wonderful evening and I don't want to spoil it by waking up in a panic, out of control. . . ."

"All right." She tried to hide her disappointment.

Clay tenderly brushed her hair back from her ear. "Tomorrow we'll have all afternoon and evening." He smiled. "Unless you have other plans?"

She returned the smile. "No other plans."

Clay switched on soft music as they drove. He held her hand. When he had to break contact to make a turn, she rested her hand on his thigh. At a stop light, they glanced at each other and he kissed her. A soft, fleeting touch of his lips. She wished he'd change his mind about taking her home with him tonight.

When they arrived at Doc's, lights blazed in the living room, kitchen, and spare bedroom. Paige murmured, "That's unusual."

Clay hopped out of the Blazer and came around to open her door. "Let's find out what's going on."

The door was standing open. Paige unlatched the screen door and they stepped inside.

Doc was sitting in his recliner, reading the newspaper. He looked up. But before he could say anything, a woman came into the living room.

Paige took a step back. It was her mother.

THIRTEEN

Paige recovered quickly and went to hug her mother. Monica returned the hug with a tight squeeze. "It's good to see you, honey. I missed you."

Monica leaned away and Paige studied her mother. Her hair was short in an easy-care style. It was the same dark brown as Paige's but liberally laced with gray. She wore jeans and a cotton blouse, her usual uniform.

Paige remembered Clay standing behind her. "Mom, this is Clay Reynolds."

Clay stepped forward and extended his hand. "It's good to meet you, Mrs. Conrad."

Monica looked him over thoroughly, then her gaze returned to Paige. "It seems like you've been out on the town."

"Clay took me out to dinner."

"I see." Monica tilted her head and examined Clay again as if searching for answers.

To break the sudden silence, Paige said, "I didn't expect you for another week."

Monica shrugged and brought her attention back to her daughter. "I finished up business sooner than I'd expected. I found half a dozen interested doctors to volunteer for six-month stints. I can do all the paperwork here while I visit with you. I thought we could leave at the end of the week.''

The end of the week. Leave Langley. Leave Clay. ''I can't.''

''What do you mean you can't?''

Paige glanced at Clay, then at Doc. She wasn't prepared for this. She wasn't prepared to make her decision. But the two men in her world didn't come to her aid. She latched on to the first excuse she could think of. ''I'm involved in planning the Fourth of July Celebration. I can't leave before that.''

Monica gave Doc a speculative look. ''That's a week and a half away. I was hoping to be in New York by then.''

Paige wasn't budging on this. ''You can go on ahead if you have to.''

Monica studied her daughter carefully. ''No, I don't think so. I'll wait until you're ready. I can make phone calls and arrange for supplies from here. But I do wonder if Doc wants me underfoot that long. I can get a room somewhere—''

''Nonsense, Monica,'' Doc finally said, moving his newspaper from his lap and folding it. ''You and Charles and Paige used to stay here on your furloughs. I'm at the office almost as much as Paige is now, and we'll both be in and out. You'll be here most of the time by yourself.''

Monica smiled. ''I do hope we'll have some time to visit.''

Paige hazarded a glance at Clay and wondered what he was thinking.

His expression was inscrutable as he said, ''I'd better be getting home. Mrs. Conrad, it was good to meet you.''

Monica gave him a curt nod.

''I'll walk you out,'' Paige decided. She couldn't let him leave without knowing what he was thinking—or without a kiss or a touch.

She and Clay walked to the Blazer in silence. Finally he asked, "What are you going to tell her?"

Why did she feel like a child still longing for her mother's approval? "I don't know."

His voice was harsh in the darkness. "Does this mean I won't be seeing you?"

The words rushed out before she had time to think about them. "No. Absolutely not. Clay, this doesn't change anything between us. It just means I have to make some time for my mother, too."

His tone lowered, gentled. "What about tomorrow?"

She wanted her mother to get to know Clay. She wanted him to get to know her mother. "Why don't you come over for brunch? Then you and I will have the afternoon together. Tomorrow evening I can spend with my mother."

"All right."

He was so removed, so stoic. "Clay, I still want to be with you."

He clasped her shoulders. "And I want to be with you." He bent his head, surrounded her with his arms, and with his kiss told her exactly how much.

Eight days later, Monica came into Paige's bedroom as she dressed for her day with Clay and his family. Paige had bought a rose-colored gauzy dress with a peasant top and full skirt when she'd purchased the fancier sundress for their dinner date. These were the first two impractical dresses she'd ever owned.

As Paige faced the mirror and put on her mother-of-pearl earrings, her mother sat on the bed. "You look nice."

"Thank you."

"Paige, this thing with you and Clay Reynolds—it's not serious, is it?"

The time had arrived. They'd skirted this issue all week. Paige would come home from her time spent with Clay to her mother's ideas and hopes for the future. Monica hadn't asked questions, just assumed Paige would fall in with her plans. As her mother had spoken of new programs, the reality of Africa came back. The needy people, the children, where Paige fit into the scheme of healing. It beckoned to her. But so did Clay. She wasn't any closer to a decision now than she'd been a week ago.

Clay hadn't questioned her, either. They hadn't discussed it. They'd spent most of their time making love.

"Yes, it's serious," Paige answered, not sure herself what that meant for any of them.

"He's not right for you."

"How can you know that? You've only seen him a few times." And each one of those times, Clay had been polite to Monica, and Monica had been polite to Clay. Conversation had never gone below the surface.

"You need to be with someone who shares your dreams. Not a small-town store owner who can't see beyond the state's boundaries."

Paige sat on the bed next to her mother. "I thought you were a better judge of character than that."

Monica lifted her chin in the regal gesture Paige knew well. "I *am* a good judge of character."

Paige usually deferred to her mother, but not this time. "There's a strength and depth to Clay you know nothing about."

Monica hopped up and paced the room. "No, what I think there is—is a physical attraction between the two of you. You're infatuated with it . . . and him."

"You're wrong. I love him."

That stopped Monica in her tracks. "You can't. You've known him only two months."

Paige folded her hands in her lap.

Monica shook her head. "You're being foolish. I just hope for all our sakes you're taking precautions."

"Mother!"

"I'm a doctor, Paige. Just because you're my daughter doesn't mean I'm blind."

Paige felt sad and disappointed her mother truly didn't realize the issue before them. It wasn't only Clay. "I was hoping you'd understand."

Monica impatiently flicked her hair behind her ear. "What am I supposed to understand?"

"That I don't know if I want to go back to Africa."

The silence in the bedroom was too heavy to weigh. Finally Monica said, "You can't be serious."

"I don't know if I'm serious. I need time to find out."

Her mother moved closer to the bed. "Honey, you were under a strain. You were vulnerable when you came here. Clay took advantage of that—"

"He took advantage of nothing. Mom, did you ever think that maybe I'm not cut out for the same life as you?"

"That's ridiculous! You fit right in, you travel well."

"I've never known anything else."

Monica waved her hand in exasperation. "Paige, I have to make up schedules, assignments, itineraries. Go back with me. See if Clay Reynolds is so important to you once you're away from him."

That was an option. But did she want to consider it?

Clay took a stuffed mushroom from the buffet table in the dining room and popped it into his mouth. Paige was on the other side of the room talking with Trish. The two women had connected right away. They were discussing something intently now and he wondered what it was.

Paige had been quieter than usual on their drive here. Because of his conversation with Doc, Clay was hesitant to poke or push. But it was evident she was troubled and so was he. The few times he'd spent with Monica Conrad, he'd realized what a strong woman she was and how much she influenced her daughter. In a way, Paige looked to her mother for her own identity.

When he made love with Paige now, some of the joy was missing. The passion was as strong as ever, but desperation had taken joy's place.

He crossed to Paige and casually curled his arm around her waist. "Are you two hatching a plot?"

Trish laughed, smoothing her hand over the hips of her yellow linen dress. "Hardly. I was telling Paige about our honeymoon plans to Hawaii. But now I have to mingle or Mom will have my head for not spending enough time with the relatives. I'll talk to you later." Trish went to the French doors and let herself outside onto the patio, where more guests were gathered.

"I can see why you love her so much," Paige said.

"In a sense, she helped me recreate my world. I wish I could remember growing up with her." Paige's hand on his arm was the balm he needed. How would he feel when she wasn't around to touch him?

"I haven't had much opportunity to speak with your mom."

Clay chuckled. "When she throws a shindig like this, she tries to be three places at one time. And usually manages it. Let me show you the rest of the house. Maybe we can find her and slow her down for a few minutes."

The house was grander than any Paige had ever seen. Hardwood floors gleamed. The rooms were spacious and elegantly furnished with mostly traditional cherry pieces. Clay led her into a small parlor decorated with a Victorian flavor—ecru lace curtains and high-back cut-velvet chairs.

"This is lovely, Clay."

He turned her to face him. "Not as lovely as you are. It's nice to get you alone."

She smiled. "You didn't really want to show me the house?"

He lifted her chin with his knuckle. "Sidetracking the tour seemed like a good idea." When he touched his lips to hers, the passion that always burst when they kissed had his heart racing, his tie tightening. He lifted his head and took a deep breath. "We should have gone *upstairs*."

"With a party going on?" she asked breathlessly.

He caressed her cheek. "We'd have our own party."

As a surge of voices swept down the hall, Clay cocked his head. "I think I hear Mom. Wait here. I'll go steal her away from the crowd."

Paige was staring out the window at the manicured lawn, the perfectly trimmed hedge, the impeccable gardens, when she heard footsteps.

She turned and came face-to-face with Vincent Reynolds. She'd met him briefly when she first arrived, but then in the crowd of thirty or more, she hadn't seen him again. She wondered about this man who had caused Clay so much pain. He'd found himself in an extraordinary situation, too, but that didn't excuse his attitude all these years later.

She wasn't sure what to say to him. "You have a beautiful home."

He nodded. "Thank you. Unfortunately, I'm not here as much as I'd like to be to enjoy it."

An awkward silence fell between them. Vincent cleared his throat. "My wife tells me you're a doctor."

"Yes, I am."

"Was Clay one of your patients?"

"No, we met through a mutual friend."

Vincent shrugged. "I was just surprised Clay was dating a doctor. Your occupation doesn't seem compatible with his."

Lord, Vincent Reynolds and her mother belonged on the same boat. The anger she'd found herself capable of since coming to Langley raised its head. "We're people, Mr. Reynolds. What we choose to do for a living is not the sum total of who we are."

He looked taken aback. "But a profession carries with it certain prerequisites—educational background for one, social stratum for another."

She tried to keep her temper. "That's not always true. And even if it were, those things don't determine what a person is inside."

He studied her for a moment. "You sound very much like Clay."

His statement implied criticism. "Is there something wrong with that?"

He sighed. "I suppose not."

She knew she was overstepping her bounds but didn't care. She might be gone in a week. Maybe she could do something for Clay. "Mr. Reynolds, do you know your son?"

"Excuse me?"

"Do you really know Clay as he is today? Do you know that he's a good, compassionate, caring man? Do you know that he's a business success? Do you know how much he needs your acceptance?"

"He doesn't need anything from me," Vincent said bitterly, stuffing his hand in his pocket. "He's made that clear. He makes sure he keeps his distance."

Nothing Vincent Reynolds could have said could have made her more angry. She knew Clay longed for a relationship with his father. Vincent must be blind not to realize it. "And just why do you think he keeps his distance? Why would he want to be around you when you can't accept him for who he is but only for what you expected him to be?" She couldn't believe she'd said that. But it was the truth as Clay saw it.

"She's right, Dad." Trish came into the room, her high heels clicking on the parquet floor. "None of us have ever had the guts to say it to you. God knows, Clay's tried. Don't you think it's time to put the past where it belongs? Forget about the family albums and get to know the son you have now?"

Vincent glanced from one woman to the other and looked defeated. "Clay and I can't talk."

"Maybe that's because you don't know how to listen," Trish offered bluntly.

Vincent was quiet for a few moments. "All these years I've been hanging on to the hope Clay would come back to the business."

Paige took a few steps closer to the man who Clay felt had rejected him at every turn. "Instead of being part of your business, wouldn't it be better if he was part of your life?"

Vincent looked at his daughter. "I do have *you* in the business."

"Yes, you do."

"I suppose I could think about making you a partner."

Trish gave a frustrated sound of disapproval. "I don't care about being your partner. I *do* care about being your daughter. Can't you see the difference, Dad?"

He grimaced. "I'm trying." He focused his attention on Paige. "Do you always fight for people you care about?"

"I wasn't aware I was fighting."

Vincent smiled. "I think Clay's a lucky man." He left the room as quietly as he'd come in.

Paige shook her head. "I don't believe I did that."

Trish grinned. "Love makes us do crazy things. And if I didn't know it when you arrived, I know it now. You love my brother."

Paige felt heat rise to her cheeks. "Yes, I do. But I haven't told him. I don't know if I'll be staying here."

"Clay told me. You have a tough decision to make."

"Did you ever want the best of both worlds?"

"All the time. But more than anything, I've learned if I don't follow my heart, I can't be happy."

The early-evening sun was still bright as Paige tossed her water balloon to Clay and glanced around to see who was watching the competition. It seemed most of the town had gathered for the Fourth of July. Everyone wore smiles and T-shirts and a collection of baseball caps. The softball game had taken most of the afternoon. She and Clay had gotten something to eat and decided to enter the balloon toss.

Clay stepped a few more feet away from Paige, grinned, and carefully tossed the balloon. She held her breath as she caught it. It didn't break.

She hadn't seen that grin of his since before her mother arrived. Even when they made love there was tension between them. She knew she was the cause.

Trish had advised her to follow her heart. Did that mean staying with Clay? Standing beside him? He hadn't even said he loved her. "More than physical" didn't necessarily mean permanent. Was she ready to risk life as she knew it for a life she knew nothing about? Was she waiting for some sign, for Clay to tell her he loved her? Then what?

Underhanded, she carefully threw the balloon back to him, the new children's immunization program planned for Zaire clicking through her head. It would save so many lives. Didn't she want to be part of it?

Clay caught the balloon, moved back, and tossed it again. This time, when she reached for it, her fingernail stabbed it and water splashed through her hands. Luckily, most of it went on her sneakers, rather than her shorts.

Clay came to her, smiling at the water dripping down her bare thigh. "Need a towel?"

"It will dry. What do you want to do next?"

"The pie-eating contest starts soon. We could head over that way."

Paige was surprised at the amount of people who waved at them and shouted hello as they made their way across the expansive field where most of the day's events were taking place. She felt as if she belonged here, as if she'd made friends.

As they approached the canopy shielding long tables from the sun, she saw Ben slap another teenage boy on the back as he settled himself at the table, ready to compete. A pretty girl with curly brown hair looked on.

Ben saw them, took the girl by the hand, and met Clay and Paige at the edge of the tent. His smile was broad, his face excited. "I want you to meet someone. This is Christy Jacobs. Christy, this is Mr. Reynolds and Dr. Conrad."

The girl smiled shyly. "It's nice to meet you."

"Christy lives in Westminster," Ben explained. "We met at an orientation meeting up at Penn State. She's going to be going there, too."

Clay clapped Ben's shoulder. "That's great news. What are you going to study?"

"I'm trying biology. Christy's going to be an elementary school teacher."

Ben was beaming, and Paige could see he was looking toward the future instead of regretting the past. "I wish you both all the luck in the world. You have bright futures."

The wide smile left Ben's face, and he became serious for the moment. "And new dreams."

Emotion tightened Paige's throat. "You've come a long way, Ben, and I'm proud of you."

His face flushed, but he said, "I have you two to thank."

Rousing cheers signaled the start of the pie-eating contest. Ben said, "We have to coach Randy. I'll be surprised if he can get one pie down. We'll see you around."

Clay put his arm around Paige's shoulders. She lay her head against his chest, and he gave her a little squeeze. "He's going to be all right."

"You had a lot to do with that."

Clay smiled. "So we can both pat ourselves on the back."

"Paige?"

Their tender moment was interrupted as Paige turned around and faced her mother. "Hi, Mom. Are you having fun?"

Monica shrugged. "It's all very interesting. I'd forgotten what these small-town get-togethers are like. I suppose you're staying for the fireworks?''

"Yes. The band's giving a concert first. Have you taken a balloon ride?" Paige had packed her fears in her back pocket first thing that morning and had soared through the heavens with Clay. It was an experience she'd remember always. Just like everything else she'd experienced with Clay during the time she'd spent in Langley.

"No balloon ride. I'll leave that to younger adventurers. I just wanted to tell you I'm going back to Doc's. I have some overseas calls to make.''

"It might be late when I get in.''

Monica's gaze moved to Clay. "I know where you'll be.''

Paige sighed as her mother walked away. "I'm sorry if she's cool to you.''

"She thinks I'm a threat.'' He paused for a moment, then asked, "Am I?''

Paige closed her eyes, so confused she couldn't think. The pull of her former life, her former dedication, her former dreams yanked against her love for Clay. She opened her eyes and stared straight ahead. "I can't answer that.''

His tone was troubled. "You have to answer it soon.''

"I know.'' The words came out in a whisper.

Clay looked as if he was going to say something, but then changed his mind. "Let's go watch the kids on the rides until the band starts playing.''

Paige let the burden of deciding slip from her as Clay's green eyes embraced her. She'd been given a reprieve and she was going to take advantage of it.

A short time later, Clay went to get them lemonade as Paige set up their lawn chairs on the football field in the area designated for the concert and fireworks.

She'd just sat in her chair when Ron Murphy unfolded his and placed it beside her. He tipped his Stetson. "The day's turned out fine and dandy, hasn't it? We even sold out of T-shirts. The committee did a grand job."

She smiled. "You did a great job of coordinating it."

He set his hat farther back on his head. "I was talking to Ben Hockensmith's mom earlier. She thinks the world of you and Clay."

"Ben's a good kid."

Ron shifted in his chair. "She told me about Clay's amnesia."

Uh-oh. Paige had never thought about telling Ben to keep his knowledge to himself.

"It's something, isn't it?" Ron went on. "Not being able to remember anything before his accident. It took guts for Clay to start all over here in Langley. I don't know if I could have done that."

"Clay's a strong man."

"Sure must be. He was always so tight-mouthed about his life before he came here. I should have suspected something, but I never would have guessed something like amnesia."

Clay handed Paige a cup of lemonade and said to Ron, "It's not as rare as people think."

She hadn't heard Clay walk up behind her. She didn't know what to say.

Ron said, "I was just telling Paige, here, how I admire your gumption." He stood. "That lemonade looks awfully good. I think I'll get some before things start popping."

Clay sat next to Paige, silent and frowning. He took a swallow of lemonade, then asked in a low voice, "Why did you tell him when you know how I feel? I thought you understood I don't want people staring at me, gossiping."

Paige felt as if he'd slapped her. How could he think she'd betray his trust? "I didn't tell him anything."

"Then how did he find out?"

"Ben's mother. Apparently she's grateful for the way you helped her son."

Paige's expression must have shown her hurt. Clay took her hand and said, "I'm sorry. I just assumed—"

"Why? How could you possibly think I'd tell Ron?"

"Maybe because I don't know how you feel."

Now was the time to say it. And to see what would happen. "I love you, Clay."

He took a deep breath. "And what does that mean?"

"It means I don't know what to do. It means I have to give up one dream for another. It means I have to make a choice. Do you want me to stay? You haven't said it."

"You know I do."

"Just as you knew you could trust me to keep your confidence?"

Clay ached inside. He longed to tell Paige he loved her. But this wasn't just a matter of love. In a way, the decision she had to make was separate from them. He couldn't make her choose between him and her life in Africa. She had to choose whether that life in Africa was best for her physical and emotional health. She had to choose whether she wanted to change her life with or without him. He could never be her world, the outlet for her dedication and compassion. She had to decide which world was better for her.

So he couldn't tell her he loved her. He couldn't use that to sway her. They'd both regret it in the years to come. He released her hand and stared straight ahead as the band tuned their instruments.

Paige said quietly, "Maybe instead of hiding your background, you should be proud of what you've accomplished and share that pride with others. Ron admires you, he doesn't think less of you. So does Ben. So does his mother. So do I."

Clay had never thought about people admiring him. He'd figured the friends he'd made in Langley would react the same as friends in his past if they knew his history. But maybe he'd been wrong.

The one thing he knew was that he'd hurt Paige and he

never wanted to hurt her. But he wasn't sure how to bridge the gap he'd dug between them. He felt isolated as the band played one song after another. Darkness fell, and instead of the night bringing them closer, it seemed divisive. Even the stars and the moon couldn't work their magic. Clay remembered his date with Paige at the restaurant by the river. He wanted that closeness back. He wanted her back.

The display of fireworks splashed the sky again and again with colors and light. Clay glanced at Paige's profile. She didn't turn to meet his gaze.

When the last rocket flew, when the last patriotic note played, when everyone stood and folded their chairs, Clay let his sit and clasped Paige's shoulders. "Come home with me tonight."

She was stiff under his hands. "I was going to."

"No, I mean stay with me tonight. All night."

She studied his face as if she didn't believe he meant it. "You're sure?"

"I trust you, Paige. I want you with me tonight and every night until you leave, if you leave. I don't want to waste a minute of it."

She smiled, and under the lights of the football field, her eyes grew bright and shiny. She stroked the line of his jaw. "I'd love to come home with you."

Clay felt as if he'd just been handed a beautiful gift.

He took Paige to his home, and this time something was different. He'd crossed a line and he hoped she'd crossed one, too. They went through the ritual of letting Shep outside for his nightly run, locking the doors, turning off the downstairs lights. Then he took Paige's hand and led her upstairs.

Wanting the anticipation to last, hoping tonight would be special for them both, he suggested, "Let's shower together."

She smiled. "So we can conserve water?"

"No, so we can enjoy each other in a new way."

Her eyes became bluer, deeper, and her smile faded away.

He undressed her. She undressed him. He turned on the water and stepped into the tub. She stepped in beside him and pulled the shower door closed.

Clay stepped under the spray, letting it roll over his shoulders, his chest. She traded places with him and kept her eyes on his as the pinging wet nettles skimmed her neck, her breasts.

Excitement was more than a word. Need became a powerful magnet drawing them to each other. "I love you" was still a phrase he couldn't say. He stepped back and drew Paige away from the water, closer to him. Taking her sweet face between his hands, he kissed her gently before easing her lips apart with his tongue.

She didn't wait for him, but met his fervor by tasting him first. Wrapping her arms around his neck, she held on to him as if she never wanted to let him go.

Her breasts rubbed his chest, her nipples hard and ready for loving. But he couldn't release her mouth, not when he didn't know if this night might be one of their last together. He caressed her back with long, slow, slick sweeps that caused her to moan. She stroked his face as they kissed, bringing every atom of his being into full alert.

This was supposed to be a shower . . . lingering foreplay to prolong their pleasure. But much more of this and—

He dragged his lips from hers. "Paige, you're not protected. We can't keep this up."

She tightened her grasp on him. "I don't care. I want this. I want you. Now."

Her honesty shredded his last hold on control. As she arched into him, he lifted her and slid inside. She was everything he needed, everything he wanted, maybe everything he couldn't have.

But he had her in his arms now. Using the wall at his back as a bulwark, he thrust into her. She tightened her legs around his hips, milked him more thoroughly. As he thrust again, she nipped his neck and scraped her nails down his back.

He shuddered and knew release was imminent. He had to hold on longer. He drove into her again and again until she was panting and giving small cries of pleasure. He shifted her slightly and when he did, she cried out, "That's it, Clay. It's so wonderful."

He couldn't hold back. He couldn't keep from speeding toward release. He could only give and take . . . and hope.

Paige shouted his name. Seconds later, he called hers. But even in the supreme ecstasy of the moment, he realized they'd solved nothing. And in a week or less, tonight might be simply a memory.

FOURTEEN

Clay awakened just after sunrise, knowing Paige would soon be awake, too. She had rounds at the hospital this morning. Last night had been nothing short of spectacular. But what would today bring?

Paige stirred against him and opened her eyes. Tilting her head up and seeing he was awake, she smiled. "Good morning."

"Good morning."

She laid her hand along the side of his neck. "You didn't have a nightmare."

"I don't have them every night."

"I was afraid my being here might trigger something."

"Maybe your being here, in bed beside me, chased them away." She looked so lovely, gazing at him with her wide blue eyes, her hair tousled from sleep. But her beauty, inside and out, clawed at him because she might not be here tomorrow or the next day. Which meant one thing: as much as she loved mankind, she didn't love him enough.

The phone jangled on his nightstand, severing the tentative bond between them. Clay couldn't imagine who'd be calling this early. Paige's beeper on her side of the bed would have signaled an emergency.

With his arm still around her, he snatched up the phone. "Clay, this is Monica Conrad. May I speak to Paige?"

A sense of foreboding burned in the pit of Clay's stomach. Stretching the phone cord across his chest, he handed the receiver to Paige. "It's your mother."

Paige pulled away from him and sat up. He hiked himself up against the headboard. As Paige listened to her mother, he watched her expression turn serious, the sparkle leave her eyes. She glanced at Clay, then looked away. The sense of foreboding burned wider and deeper.

Finally Paige said to her mother, "I understand. I'll see you tonight." She handed the receiver to Clay, avoiding his gaze.

He set the phone down with a rough snap. "What did she want?"

Paige looked at him then, with eyes filled with misery and confusion. "She wants my decision by tonight. She says she can't wait any longer. Doc's taking her to Johns Hopkins. There's a doctor there who might be interested in our work."

Paige was still connected to her mother, to *their* work. "What have you decided?"

Tears glistened in her eyes. "I don't know."

He couldn't live in this limbo. If Paige was going, he'd have to live with that. But he needed to know. She needed to decide. "What do *you* want?"

She shook her head, unable to answer.

Unbidden, anger took the place of the foreboding. "You're a hypocrite, Paige. You told Ben to go after his dreams and you're afraid to do it yourself. Does your mother's approval mean so much more than your own happiness?"

She swayed away from him. "No, of course not. I loved the work."

His mouth twisted wryly, and he couldn't help but ask

the questions that had plagued him about her life to this point. "Did you? Or did you love your parents so much that that deluded you into thinking you had to be just like them? Love what they love. Be what they wanted you to be. Have you ever thought about you, Paige, separate from them? Have you ever imagined a life *you* forged, not them?"

"All I ever wanted to do was . . ." She looked down at her hands.

"Heal," he filled in. "And you can do that anywhere." He was going to do something he'd sworn he wouldn't do. But if there was any way he could keep her here . . . "Paige, I love you. But you have to want a life with me as much as I want one with you. Your loyalty can't be divided. If you stay and wish you'd gone, it will destroy the love we have."

A tear tripped down her cheek, wrenching his heart. "I know. If I stay, I have to forget my life in Africa, my parents' goals and dreams. But I don't know if I can. Mother suggested I go back with her, see how I feel . . ."

That suggestion fueled Clay's anger. "Out of sight, out of mind. She's hoping you'll forget me."

Paige reached for his hand. "I'll never forget you. And it might give me some time. . . ."

He eluded her touch, knowing it would be too painful right now. Swearing, he impatiently ran his hand through his hair. "All time will do is postpone the inevitable. You don't need time. You need a large dose of courage." He hadn't meant to be that harsh, but he didn't want to lose her. He'd lost too much already.

She took in a breath and her face paled. "That's not fair."

"It's the truth. And maybe it's time you looked at it. You know what you want. You're afraid to reach out and take it."

Her shoulders stiffened, and he knew he was pushing her away. But he'd taken risk after risk with her, and now it was time she take one. If she loved him enough, she would. "Do you remember what you said last night?"

"I said lots of things."

"In the shower."

Color came back to her face and her voice lowered. "I don't remember."

He went on relentlessly, trying to make her see what was evident to him. "I knew you weren't protected and I said we should stop. Your exact words were, 'I don't care. I want this. I want you. Now.' "

Her hands fluttered against the sheet. "But we were in the middle of something physical. It was just . . . I . . ."

"It was just sex? It was an impulse of the moment? I don't think so. We were making love and that was truth coming out."

"You think you know me better than I know myself."

"Maybe I do. Did you ever think that maybe you wanted to get pregnant so the problem would resolve itself? So you wouldn't have to *make* a decision?"

She flushed and looked guilty, as if that thought had occurred to her, too.

And he was angry again, disappointed, and hurt she couldn't love him with the same certainty with which he loved her. "I don't want you that way, Paige. I don't want you by default. My parents and Trish were saddled with me after the accident—the *new* Clay. It wasn't their choice. I will *not* spend the rest of my life with someone who can't freely choose to be with me. It has to be a decision, Paige. A conscious, honest decision. And if you're not ready to make it, you should go back to Africa with your mother. That would be best for both of us."

Clay flicked off the computer in his office, disgusted with himself. He couldn't concentrate. All he could think about was Paige. He'd issued an ultimatum. He'd closed a door between them. She'd left for the hospital, the climate between them cool and ambivalent.

What if she *did* need time and space? He'd made it sound that if she left with her mother he didn't want to see her again. What if she left, *then* realized she wanted a life with him? Should he shut off that hope?

Life had become complicated. But he wouldn't go back. He wouldn't have lived the last six weeks any differently if he could. Maybe Paige needed to see that his love didn't have conditions or demands.

Clay's assistant manager stuck his head into the office. "Someone's here to see you."

Maybe it was Paige. Maybe she'd made a decision. His heart hammered hard.

It wasn't Paige standing in front of the cash register. It was his father. "Dad?"

In the typical three-piece suit, lines creasing his forehead, Vincent Reynolds looked serious enough to announce a stock-market crash. Instead, he asked, "Can we talk?"

Clay motioned to his office. "Sure. Come on in." Once they were inside, he closed the door. "What's up?"

"It's Trish."

Clay's heart almost stopped. "What's wrong? Has she been hurt?"

Vincent put up his hand as if to stop Clay's worry. "No. No. Nothing like that. I, uh, I want her to have a beautiful wedding."

Clay was perplexed. "So do I. Is there something I can help with? Something you need?"

Vincent rubbed his hands together absently. "No, nothing material. What she wants is a happy day and I want to give her that."

Clay still didn't know what his father was getting at. "Of course it will be happy. Why wouldn't it be?"

"She wants us to . . . get along."

Clay finally broke the silence. "And what do you want?"

His father passed his hand across his forehead. "All

these years, I kept believing you'd change, that you'd want to come back to the business, come back to me."

Clay could hear the pain, the disappointment. But this time more than a career and a partnership were involved. He heard the underlying note of hurt caused by rejection.

"Dad, you've got to understand that when I decided to start over in Langley, I wasn't running away from you, I was running toward a new life. Can't you see the difference?"

Vincent studied his son, looking for the truth. "Maybe I can now. I couldn't then. Can you honestly tell me you didn't leave Reisterstown because of me?"

Honesty. How could he be honest without hurting his father? "I left because I needed to find myself. I was creating problems for you and Mom. Trish was spending too much time with me and didn't have a life of her own. Mom hovered, afraid to let me out of her sight. How could any of us keep going like that?"

"That's really the way you saw it?"

"Yes. Plus one more factor. I felt I was constantly disappointing you because I couldn't be the son you knew and loved before the accident."

Vincent's face expressed his sadness. "I did a poor job of hiding how I felt. How lost I felt. My life had always revolved around you, Clay. After the accident, nothing made sense."

"And what about now?" Clay asked quietly.

"I guess I behaved all these years as if I'd lost a son. Can you forgive me for that?"

"If you can forgive me for needing a fresh start."

Clay's father didn't hesitate. "Done."

"Done," Clay repeated, extending his hand.

His father then did something totally unexpected. He took Clay's hand and gave it a short tug. Clay realized his father needed his love and approval as much as he needed his father's. He hugged Vincent Reynolds for the first time in ten long years. It felt good. It felt right. And the peace that had expanded wider and wider during these past two weeks with Paige seemed to fill him until it overflowed.

Vincent stepped back and Clay could see his father was clearly embarrassed.

Clay moved to the office door and said, "You've never really seen the store and repair shop. Would you like to look around?"

His father smiled. "I'd like that a lot. I might even be persuaded to buy a new mower. *If* the price is right."

Clay smiled back. "We'll make it right."

He took his time with his father, knowing they were planting the seeds for a new relationship. But as soon as Vincent got into his car and drove away, Clay's thoughts returned to Paige.

He had to see her. He had to reopen the door between them. Clay checked his watch. She should be finished at the hospital.

Her car was in Doc's driveway. She was nowhere around. Not in the house, not on the deck. He even checked the shed. Then he remembered and decided she would, too. She would head for a haven, someplace special.

He found her sitting near the tree where they'd made love, a bluet in her hand. She was studying it as if it held all the secrets in the world, the cure for her turmoil. But when she raised her head and saw him, all the turmoil was still there.

She tried to smile. "I didn't know if I'd ever see you again."

"Paige . . ."

Before he could go to her, before he could sit down beside her, her beeper went off.

Clay swore. Talking would have to wait.

She heard his frustration, but she said, "I have to answer this."

"I know." If he understood anything about Paige, it was her dedication.

He followed her to the house and leaned against the counter while she dialed her service. Her face was concerned as she spoke to them, then dialed another number. "It's Miriam. The baby's coming. Her water broke. I have to let her know I'm on my way."

After Paige talked to Miriam, reassuring her, calming her, she made another call. But no one answered.

"What's wrong?"

"It's my nurse. She was going to assist, but I can't get an answer. Even if I leave a message, it might be too late until she gets it."

"I don't know how much help I'll be, but I can come along if you'd like."

She nodded. "I'd like that. It's always good to have another pair of hands."

Before they left, Paige called the hospital to alert them in case there were problems. Clay knew she would take every precaution where Miriam's health and her baby's were concerned.

They arrived at Miriam's in a matter of minutes. Clay watched the doctor in Paige take over as she became methodical and focused. He knew she'd already talked with Miriam at length about the process of labor and childbirth and had provided supplies they might need—such as a foam wedge to prop on, basins, sterile sheets, antiseptic, gauze pads. While Paige took Miriam's vital signs, Clay put on water to boil to sterilize the instruments in case any were needed.

When he went to the bedroom where Paige was getting Miriam comfortably settled, Miriam said to Clay, "You two should be a team."

Paige glanced his way, but he couldn't tell from her expression what she was thinking. Something else was more important right now, Miriam's well-being. He said to her, "I can help Paige, but only if you don't mind."

A contraction overtook Miriam. She concentrated on the breathing technique Paige had taught her and worked with the contraction. When it had subsided, she said, "Right now, I just want this baby born. Hell's Angels could ride through here and I wouldn't care. So if you can help Dr. Conrad, it's fine with me. Ever seen a baby born before?"

He smiled. "Not a human. I helped deliver a calf once."

Miriam laughed. "This can't be that different, right?"

Paige patted Miriam's arm. "Giving birth is a natural process. We just follow the signals. Are you sure you're comfortable?"

Propped on the wedge in a half sitting, half reclining position, Miriam answered, "As comfortable as I'm going to get. I'm not too crazy about this hospital gown you brought me."

Paige smiled. "You can worry about fashion after the baby's born. It will make things easier for me. Clay, while I check the baby's heartrate, can you get Miriam a glass of crushed ice? It's in the freezer door."

Clay paced the living room as Miriam's contractions came faster and Paige spoke to her about transition and the next stage. It was obvious Paige had prepared Miriam well, and she understood exactly what was happening to her. Paige managed and supported, reassuring Miriam all the while. But the pain of labor seemed to be something only two women could share. Unless . . .

Unless that was Paige in that bed and *his* baby being born. Was there a chance for that?

He needed something to do, so he made a pot of coffee. He was pouring himself a cup when Paige called to him to scrub with the antiseptic she'd left in the bathroom.

The coffee sloshed over the rim as he set down the cup and hurried to get ready.

He rushed to the bedroom, his hands held in front of him. Paige looked as hot and flushed as Miriam as she peered under the sheet draping Miriam's knees. "The head's crowning. A couple of good pushes and Miriam will have her child in her arms. I'll need you to hand me the washcloth and suction syringe.''

Paige felt Clay's presence beside her, his quiet assurance, his strength. When he'd told her she should go back to Africa for both their sakes, her heart had ripped in two. And all morning as she'd made her rounds, she'd told herself he was right. Her indecision was tearing them apart as effectively as her absence would.

She loved this man. But would staying in the States, developing a private practice, be enough? When would she know? Could she lose Clay until she worked it through?

She tried to put her personal life out of her mind as she readied herself for the birth. She looked at Miriam and could see another contraction was ready to hit. "Okay, Miriam. Now I want a giant push. Put all the energy you have left into this one. Take a deep breath. Okay, let's go.''

Miriam's cry mingled with the cry of new life as Paige supported the baby's head and shoulders when he emerged from his mother. Paige had done this before, many times. She had heard a baby's first cry. She had seen the ten miniature fingers. She had felt the perfect softness of a newborn's skin.

But this time, *this time* was different.

Words echoed in her head. *I want this. I want you. Now.* And she knew why the decision had been so hard to make. She'd been listening to her head, trying to be logical, trying to reason, trying to weigh and sort. She hadn't been listening to her heart.

Holding the baby in her arms, holding life in her hands, her love for Clay overwhelmed her and brought tears welling in her eyes. This is what she wanted.

She wanted to love Clay, share with Clay, live with Clay, have a family with Clay. And somehow everything else would fall into place. Because Clay was that kind of man. Somehow she'd find a balance. Beside him, with him, joined to him.

As tears ran down her cheeks, she knew she was the one who'd have to risk this time. She'd have to ask Clay if he still wanted her, if he still wanted a life with her. And she'd have to make certain he knew she had no doubts.

She lifted her head and her gaze met his. The sadness she saw there stabbed her, and suddenly she knew what he was thinking. He believed she was going back to Africa. But this moment wasn't theirs. It was Miriam's.

Clay handed her a washcloth. She wiped off the baby's face, cleaned out his mouth, and carefully checked the appearance of the newborn. He cried more vigorously.

Paige wrapped the baby and laid him on his mother's stomach. Miriam gazed at her child with love.

Clay said, "I'll wait in the living room."

His voice was strained and Paige wanted to run after him, but she wasn't finished here yet. Just a few more minutes and she could tell Clay everything that was in her heart.

When the baby lay on Miriam's chest nursing, Paige went to the living room. Clay wasn't there and she panicked. Maybe he'd left, maybe he'd decided . . .

She saw movement on the porch and went outside.

He heard the door but didn't turn around. "Are they all right?"

"Mother and baby are doing well. I have to call Miriam's neighbor. She's going to stay with her for a few days. But before I do that, I wanted to talk to you."

Clay's back was rigid, his arms stiff at his sides. "You don't have to say it. I saw it on your face."

"What did you see?"

He turned around then. "Your dedication. Your joy. I can't compete with that."

Suddenly words seemed hard to find. All she could say was, "You don't have to compete."

"You *want* to go back. I could see it—"

"No. That isn't what you saw." She had to do it. She had to do it now. She had to claim the life *she* wanted. "I want to have your children, Clay."

He stared at her until the meaning behind her words sunk in. "You want to stay here?"

"I don't think I can get pregnant long distance. At least not with the method *I* want to use." She smiled, her heart feeling light and free.

The seriousness left his eyes and he grinned. "Marriage should come before babies."

"Is that a proposal?"

He wound his arms about her and swung her off her feet. "Yes, that's a proposal. And I won't put you down until you give me an answer."

She wrapped her arms around his neck. "Yes, I'll marry you."

He squeezed her tighter. "When?"

"Tomorrow?"

He laughed. "We need a few days."

"Maybe mother will stay."

He set her on her feet and framed her face with his hands. "You're sure this is what you want? What about your mother's plans? Your dreams?"

"My dreams have changed. Now you're in them. I'm not sure what I want to do professionally. I've been hearing talk at the hospital about setting up a free clinic in the county for unwed mothers and prenatal care. I might want to get involved in that. I'm not sure. What I am sure about is that I want to stay here and start a life with you."

The love in Clay's green eyes overwhelmed her. It shook her and filled her with such awe and thankfulness, she couldn't breathe.

When he spoke, his voice was raspy with the depth of emotion he was feeling. "I love you."

She stroked his cheek and tears pricked her eyes. "I love you, too. Do you know where I'd like to get married?"

He knew immediately. "In the clearing in the woods beside the patches of wild flowers."

She nodded, because she couldn't speak. There were no more words.

Clay's lips sought hers with gentle demand yet passionate fervor. The kiss was filled with promises and wild flowers and children and everything beautiful. She was his. And he was hers. Forever.

EPILOGUE

Paige stood outside the adobe house, gazing at the rugged mountains. This small Central American country was a tropical land of mountains, volcanoes, green valleys, and natural lakes. But its rapidly growing population had almost exhausted its available supply of farmland.

That's where Clay came in. He was teaching farmers newer methods of farming and expertise with repairing machinery—old machinery and also new equipment that he'd ordered from generous private donations. Clay had learned a handful of Spanish before their first trip six months after they were married. Now, two years later, he could speak it almost as fluently as she could.

While Clay worked with the farmers, she healed, for six weeks every six months. That might have to stop now.

Her senses picked up someone approaching, and she swung around. Clay was walking up the hillside, his shirt tied around his waist. His bronze skin shimmered in the last rays of afternoon light.

She ran to meet him, her heart racing, because just the sight of him thrilled her as it had from the day they'd met.

He caught her against him and kissed her soundly. Her

pulse raced, desire sped through her, and she reveled in their physical and emotional closeness and the life they shared. But that life was about to change.

Clay ended the kiss and laughed. "I have to wash up before we continue this."

She ran her hands over his shoulders, inhaling his masculine scent, work and man and sun. "You're fine as you are."

"Keep touching me like that and I'll be even finer." He studied her face. "I can tell you've been thinking. What's going on?"

He could read her as easily as she could read him. Yet she'd been hiding something the past few weeks. Their hopes had been dashed a couple of times over the last two years, and this time she'd wanted to be sure.

"We got a letter from Doc today. He wants to take an extended vacation with Faye to make sure they're 'right' for each other."

Clay chuckled. "They've been dating a year. You'd think he'd know by now."

Paige smiled. "It's hard for him to put his confirmed-bachelor days aside. Anyway, instead of his working with me part-time and covering when I'm here, he wants me to think about taking on a partner."

"How do you feel about that?"

"I'll miss Doc terribly. But it would give me more time to work at the women's clinic and . . ."

"And?"

"And hopefully I'd have someone to cover for me if I want to spend a few weeks or a month or so off."

"Off? Are you thinking about doing more than two of these stints a year?"

"Mother would love that. But, no. I think this is enough to handle."

Love for Paige welled up and overflowed in Clay. He remembered the first time she'd come to him with the idea of working in the field for six weeks. She'd been concerned about his reaction, but he'd witnessed her excitement. The more he questioned her about it, the more he'd realized he could make a contribution, too. They could do it together. It had been good for both of them, good for their marriage, good for their souls. He hadn't had a nightmare since the first time he and Paige made love. Maybe because he'd shared his secret, maybe because of the trust they'd given to each other, maybe because of their commitment.

Paige had found her boundaries. Although Monica Conrad hadn't understood Paige's decision to stay in Langley, she hadn't been a barrier either once she'd realized she and her daughter *were* different. She'd helped Paige find her niche. For that Clay was grateful.

But now Paige was talking about a month or so off and he didn't understand why. "Do you feel you need more of a break than you get when we return home?" He smiled. "Or are we planning a second honeymoon? Shep loves staying with Doc and taking his runs in the woods while we're gone."

"I think we've lost our chance for a second honeymoon for a while. I'm pregnant, Clay."

The news sped to his head like a jigger of aged whiskey. After a stunned moment, he grabbed her by the arms. "Are you okay? Should we be here? Maybe we should go home."

She stroked her fingers across his cheekbone. "I'm fine. Every day I teach women how to take care of themselves and their unborn children."

"This isn't just a missed period?" Their traveling had thrown Paige's cycle off more than once, and they'd been disappointed when she wasn't pregnant.

Her voice now was certain, her blue eyes sure. "No. I tested myself this morning. I'm pregnant, Clay. We're going to have a baby."

He gathered her into his arms and held her for a long

time. His throat constricted; he'd never realized he could love another person this much.

He remembered something he'd seen when he'd climbed the hillside. Kissing her temple, he found his voice and said gently, "Don't move. I'll be right back."

An inner whisper told Paige she'd heard those words before. She smiled. She'd discovered Clay was a gift giver. Before they were married, she'd told him she wanted a simple gold band. He'd given her that, plus an elegant pearl and diamond ring to wear when she wasn't working. He often brought her surprises, a special blend of tea, a silk scarf that he said matched her eyes, a sweater she'd admired in a shop window. But she appreciated one gift most of all. She suspected Clay knew that.

He'd disappeared over the crest of the hill and reappeared a few minutes later. In his hand, he held a bouquet of wild flowers—stems of tiny white petals, pink lacy fronds, cornflower-blue cups.

He offered them to her and she took them reverently into her hands, appreciating the delicate petals, the colors, the lingering scent. Appreciating Clay. "Do you know how much I love you?"

He smiled. "If I counted each and every wild flower on the earth, would I get the idea?"

"You'd get the idea."

With the bouquet of wild flowers in one hand, the other one free to play in Clay's hair, she kissed him and felt the depth and breadth and magnitude of her love returned. Their love would bloom and grow in the years to come. She thought about holding their child in her arms, and then she let herself drown in their passion and love.

Clay lifted Paige into his arms, gazed into her eyes, carried her into the adobe house. And then he kissed her again.

SHARE THE FUN . . .
SHARE YOUR NEW-FOUND TREASURE!!

You don't want to let your new books out of your sight? That's okay. Your friends can get their own. Order below.

No. 74 A MAN WORTH LOVING by Karen Rose Smith
Nate's middle name is 'freedom' . . . that is, until Shara comes along.

No. 100 GARDEN OF FANTASY by Karen Rose Smith
If Beth wasn't careful, she'd fall into the arms of her enemy, Nash.

No. 140 LOVE IN BLOOM by Karen Rose Smith
Clay has no past that he can remember. Can he make a future with Paige?

No. 66 BACK OF BEYOND by Shirley Faye
Dani and Jesse are forced to face their true feelings for each other.

No. 67 CRYSTAL CLEAR by Cay David
Max could be the end of all Chrystal's dreams . . . or just the beginning!

No. 68 PROMISE OF PARADISE by Karen Lawton Barrett
Gabriel is surprised to find that Eden's beauty is not just skin deep.

No. 69 OCEAN OF DREAMS by Patricia Hagan
Is Jenny just another shipboard romance to Officer Kirk Moen?

No. 70 SUNDAY KIND OF LOVE by Lois Faye Dyer
Trace literally sweeps beautiful, ebony-haired Lily off her feet.

No. 71 ISLAND SECRETS by Darcy Rice
Chad has the power to take away Tucker's hard-earned independence.

No. 72 COMING HOME by Janis Reams Hudson
Clint always loved Lacey. Now Fate has given them another chance.

No. 73 KING'S RANSOM by Sharon Sala
Jesse was always like King's little sister. When did it all change?

No. 75 RAINBOWS & LOVE SONGS by Catherine Sellers
Dan has more than one problem. One of them is named Kacy!

No. 76 ALWAYS ANNIE by Patty Copeland
Annie is down-to-earth and real . . . and Ted's never met anyone like her.

No. 77 FLIGHT OF THE SWAN by Lacey Dancer
Rich had decided to swear off romance for good until Christiana.

No. 78 TO LOVE A COWBOY by Laura Phillips
Dee is the dark-haired beauty that sends Nick reeling back to the past.

No. 79 SASSY LADY by Becky Barker
No matter how hard he tries, Curt can't seem to get away from Maggie.

No. 80 CRITIC'S CHOICE by Kathleen Yapp
Marlis can't do one thing right in front of her handsome houseguest.

No. 81 TUNE IN TOMORROW by Laura Michaels
Deke happily gave up life in the fast lane. Can Liz do the same?

No. 82 CALL BACK OUR YESTERDAYS by Phyllis Houseman
Michael comes to terms with his past with Laura by his side.

No. 83 ECHOES by Nancy Morse
Cathy comes home and finds love even better the second time around.

No. 84 FAIR WINDS by Helen Carras
Fate blows Eve into Vic's life and he finds he can't let her go.

No. 85 ONE SNOWY NIGHT by Ellen Moore
Randy catches Scarlett fever and he finds there's no cure.

No. 86 MAVERICK'S LADY by Linda Jenkins
Bentley considered herself worldly but she was not prepared for Reid.

No. 87 ALL THROUGH THE HOUSE by Janice Bartlett
Abigail is just doing her job but Nate blocks her every move.

Meteor Publishing Corporation
Dept. 493, P. O. Box 41820, Philadelphia, PA 19101-9828

Please send the books I've indicated below. Check or money order (U.S. Dollars only)—no cash, stamps or C.O.D.s (PA residents, add 6% sales tax). I am enclosing $2.95 plus 75¢ handling fee for *each* book ordered.

Total Amount Enclosed: $_____.

____ No. 74	____ No. 69	____ No. 76	____ No. 82
____ No. 100	____ No. 70	____ No. 77	____ No. 83
____ No. 140	____ No. 71	____ No. 78	____ No. 84
____ No. 66	____ No. 72	____ No. 79	____ No. 85
____ No. 67	____ No. 73	____ No. 80	____ No. 86
____ No. 68	____ No. 75	____ No. 81	____ No. 87

Please Print:
Name _____
Address _____ Apt. No. _____
City/State _____ Zip _____

Allow four to six weeks for delivery. Quantities limited.